LANCASHIRE
HEADQUARTER
THIS BOOK SHOULD BE RE
DATE SHOWN TO THE LIBR

D0351663

GEAC

5l

22 03 1992
80.

08. 03. 93

LEYLAND

SK 8/94

KIRKFOLD
TEL: (0772)
744457

24. JAN 1995

AUTHOR

PRESSBURGER, G.

CLASS

F - G

TITLE

21 09 93

Homage to the eighth district

Lancashire
County
Council

THE LANCASHIRE LIBRARY.
Library Headquarters,
143, Corporation St.,
PRESTON PR1 2TB.

a30118 044463655b

COUNTY LIBRARY

Giorgio and Nicola Pressburger

Homage
to the
Eighth District

Tales from Budapest

translated by Gerald Moore

readers international

This book was first published in Italy in 1986 under the title
Storie dell'Ottavo Distretto by Casa Editrice Marietti, Genoa.
© Casa Editrice Marietti S.p.A. 1986

First published in English by Readers International Inc,
Columbia, Louisiana USA and Readers International, London.
Editorial inquiries to the London office at 8 Strathray Gardens,
London NW3 4NY England. US/Canadian inquiries to the
Subscriber Service Dept, P.O.Box 959, Columbia LA 71418 USA.

English translation © Readers International Inc 1990
All rights reserved

04446365 5

Cover illustration: *Father and Uncle Piacsek Drinking Red Wine*,
1907, by the Hungarian artist József Rippl-Rónai. Courtesy of the
Hungarian National Gallery, Budapest
Cover design by Jan Brychta
Printed and bound in Malta by Interprint Limited

Library of Congress Catalog Card Number: 89-64269

British Library Cataloguing in Publication Data
Pressburger, Giorgio *1937* -
    Homage to the eighth district: tales from Budapest.
    1. Short stories in Italian. Hungarian writers.
    I. Title   II. Pressburger, Nicola, *1937-1985*
    III. Storie dell'Ottavo Distretto. *English*
    853

ISBN 0-930523-75-X Hardcover
ISBN 0-930523-76-8 Paperback

SL ......   SL-P ......
SA ......   SO 9/92
SB ......   SP 4/9A
SK ......   SY ......

Contents

Homage to the Eighth District

The tourist who sets out to visit Budapest, a principal city of an empire non-existent for over half a century, but still remembered for the gaiety of its leading citizens and the multiplicity of its peoples, could stumble upon the Eighth District only by mistake.

Getting down at the East Station, he would have to meander along one of the narrowest and darkest ways, all cobbled with granite, which open off Ràkòczy Avenue, to the left of those leading towards the city centre.

There he will find no monuments, no famous sites nor vivacious *quartiers*. Peeling facades, still bearing traces of their original decor, but untouched for almost a century, will greet him with indifference; and the people coming and going through the entrances or along the street will appear no less indifferent, even though bearing in their eyes strange lamps of anxiety. This is no place to visit with a light heart, but with one full of suffering, of sadness, even of abjection. After following several streets, however, the visitor might come across large squares filled with trees: for the Eighth District was created, towards the end of the last century, as a clean and spacious quarter, ready to offer dignified comfort to its bourgeois inhabitants. The urban planners of the time had conceived of it almost as an ideal

1

city, tracing out its generous limits with certain destinations well defined. On one side of the district was chosen the site for a big cemetery, which was soon crammed with thousands upon thousands of tombs, some of monumental proportions, and with pompous mausolea for the Fathers of the Nation. Two other sides were to be flanked by important thoroughfares, fundamental to the layout of Budapest itself: Ràkòczy Avenue for one; and the other, one of the ring roads that start at the Danube and finally return to it. The fourth side was left open to offer room for the later development of factories, shops and other commerce.

In the middle of the District, the spacious Colomanno Tisza Square, with its green lawns and plentiful stone benches, should have become a spiritual centre, so to speak, thanks to the proximity of the City Theatre. But this theatre was to arise only several decades later, becoming one of the principal houses of the city, able to hold more than two thousand spectators. Not far from this square lay the hospital complex, consisting of one red brick edifice and another, constructed later, with a more modern finish in green tiles. The presence of good health facilities was thus ensured. The brick building, boasting an impressive tower and a rotating elevator of separate cubicles, nicknamed Pater Noster for its resemblance to a gigantic rosary, was the seat of the National Social Security offices.

Not far from Colomanno Tisza Square, the architects had designed another open space, named Teleky Square, destined to be a market because of its excellent location, near to the supply routes for provisions from outside the city and to the traders coming from the centre. And it was this very square which was destined to infect, over the coming years, all the rest of the new district and to give it an aspect little dreamed of by any of the illustrious planners of the future Budapest. The market, in fact, immediately drew in a large number of Jewish traders: junk dealers, grocers, moneylenders, and the inevitable taverners, always ready to ply with drink the peasants come to town to sell their wares. All this mob gradually penetrated the fabric of the houses, occupying the basements and the darkest rooms of the ground floors. The inhabitants of the upper floors (petit bourgeois, decadent nobles, conformists, patriots, landlords) soon took flight; and the big houses - built pretentiously with vast rooms, floral decorations, stucco mouldings, ornamental facades - were soon adapted to their new population. The buildings were divided up to form little hives of one-room apartments, with no conveniences or any of those hygienic services that urban life nowadays provides for all those having a little dignity. The Jewish traders from the basement thus climbed at last to the very highest floors.

By the beginning of the twentieth century of the Christian era, the Eighth District of Budapest was already occupied by tens of thousands of Jews and Gypsies, those two rejected minorities of the Austro-Hungarian Empire, whilst Teleky Square, with kiosks and stalls jammed into every inch, had become a by no means insignificant centre of business, as well as a crucible of poverty and human suffering - that poverty and that suffering which spring up soon enough and of which no one can see the end.

3

THE SHADOW

Sundays were dedicated to family visits. In the mornings my brothers and I got moving about ten o'clock to go and greet our grandmother, our uncles and aunts, who all lived more or less within the Eighth District, a few blocks distant from one another and from us. Our family was the most numerous, and we children acted as messengers for the grown-ups. Wherever we arrived, we were first of all asked news of our parents and of anything that had befallen our household during the week. Then followed questions about all the other households, all the uncles and aunts whom we had already visited. At the end, together with a little loose change, we would be charged with a message for some relative still to be visited. These were poor houses of humble folk, who were content to scoop themselves a little hole in the body of the city, an apartment consisting of scarcely one room, with a kitchen. This could suffice for some of them, like Aunt Leila, who had no children. But sometimes several generations lived together in the same room. My great-grandfather, for instance, lived with his daughter and her husband and child. All lived around the great centre of business, the market, where stalls selling every type of goods, from foodstuffs to clothing, from tools to old shoes, filled a square mile of land, all dust in the summer and all mud in the winter. The houses to be visited lay within a few dozen yards of this arena. I still remember the string of kitchens and living rooms, each with its own odour, and the emergence of uncles or aunts from the shadows, always with a welcoming smile in response to our greetings. Every house also had its own character, calm, joyful or irritable, according to the character of its occupants.

After the war the scene had changed. My relatives still lived near the great market. But they were in better apartments, of two or three rooms, and lying more distant from one another. The population of the quarter was frighteningly reduced by the Holocaust of the Jews, and there was much more space for the survivors. My own family had advanced a step up the scale of human and social dignity. But we boys, now about ten years old, still preserved our role as messengers. Every Sunday morning we left our house, also larger and lighter than our previous abode, to make our round of visits, rather longer now that our relatives were more dispersed around the quarter. This fell strictly on Sunday mornings. Not on Saturday, the proper Sabbath of the Jews, because the humble traders of my city had long since had to adopt the Christian calendar.

On Sunday afternoons the roles were reversed. Our family was the one to receive visits. I don't know if this was also part of the unwritten order of things, but whereas in the morning we maintained contact with my mother's relatives, in the afternoon it was those of my father who came to seek us out. It was a rather thinner procession than that of the morning, for my father's family had been decimated by the persecutions. Vanished at Auschwitz or at Bergen Belsen were the grandparents and the two uncles; there remained only a brother of my grandfather's, Uncle Gustav, and his children, Emmeric and Ella.

I don't recall the first occasion on which Erika, Ella's daughter, came to visit us; the moment is irretrievably lost in the time of childhood. I know only that Erika, whose Jewish name was Zilla, shadow (following the custom of double names, one for official use and the other for our community), immediately became the great, marvellous, ineffable delight of my Sundays. Lunch once over, my heart expected nothing but the arrival of Aunt Ella, who came to see not us (well educated and well married, she would not have descended so far in the social scale), but her father, our regular visitor on Sundays and for a while also our lodger. Sometimes it happened that I waited in vain; a phone call from Ella would cancel the appointment and Emmeric would appear in her stead. He was a sarcastic engineer, intelligent and amusing, but with the great defect of not possessing a daughter like Zilla.

My joy was all the greater when she did come. As I remember her, she wore a white blouse buttoned up to the chin, a blue skirt and white stockings up to her knees. With long black hair gathered in plaits and big dark eyes, perhaps Zilla would not have possessed any special beauty (on our upper floor little Ida had blonde hair, blue eyes and a mysterious look) had it not been for her mouth and her smile.

She had a red mouth made exactly to one's dreams, shaped for expressing joy. And when she smiled - in speaking, she smiled always - it was as if a happy light

7

shone also from her eyes and even from her two plaits, which fell down over her breast. "What a beautiful mouth you have," I said to her once when, seated on the sofa side by side, I reached my palm up to her cheek. I spoke loudly, not having the least shame before the people all around us.

"You too are beautiful," she replied, with her illuminating smile.

"But listen to them, just listen," exclaimed Ella, who was sitting near us and sipping a gooseberry fool prepared by my mother, "listen to the lovers!" I was not the least bit put out. But I saw my mother's face darken a moment, in a sorrowful grimace which mingled horror, jealousy and fear.

I felt my mother's look pierce me like a thorn. I realized it was only a pretext when she sent me to the kitchen to fetch mineral water for the guests. When I returned, I found her sitting on the sofa in my place, chatting with Zilla, all smiling and gracious. We were not able to get close together again that day, and from then on, we never exchanged compliments in front of the others. We realized it would be perilous. I was my mother's favourite, the son who, when she felt a terrible headache descend in the evening, would massage her temples, then pull off her shoes, and sometimes even follow her to bed, changing cold compresses on her brow till late in the evening, falling asleep like that, she upon her back and I with one arm around her. Apart from the pleasure it gave her, this tender attachment of mine, as I discovered later, was the more welcome because of the hatred she already felt for the whole male sex, my father most of all, owing to the wrongs

8

and betrayals she had suffered. Because I don't believe she was jealous. My mother did not fail to propose for me, part in earnest, part in jest, possible girlfriends or fiancées. But they were all bloodless girls, gloomy and insignificant, without a trace of that effervescence which Erika gave off every moment. In essence what my mother was trying to administer to me was the exact copy of her own experience with the opposite sex: a sickly and acrid relationship, a guarantee of unhappiness. She simply wanted to assure herself that we children should in the future be quite as wretched as she, married at twenty, immediately made pregnant, and probably deceived by my father before the children were even born. The horror I had glimpsed in her eyes that afternoon must have been of this very origin. A happy relationship in love was for her something to be reproved, to be stifled; because love deceived, embittered and betrayed was, from her own personal experience, the only legitimate one. The child of ten could not reconstruct this terrible logic in a mother's soul. He could only divine that his delight in being close to Zilla was in some way disapproved of and found execrable by the very person who was closest to his heart.

Mother's disapprobation was not long in showing itself even more openly. A few Sundays later the girl visited us again, and I wouldn't for anything in the world quit my place beside her. While Ella, Uncle Gustav and my parents talked, I played with Zilla's plaits. I kept loosening and undoing them, for sheer mischief. And she laughingly redid them every time. Then for a few minutes, we held hands, pretending to play. I felt a delicious warmth flow into me through her small fingers, making me gay and courageous.

9

I was ravished by this sensation, felt by me for the first time in my life, and perhaps the last. I greeted it like a marvellous gift from the universe, the welcoming gesture of the world which hitherto had been hidden from me by the heavy shadow cast by my parents. I longed to fling open the front door and run downstairs, out into the street, into the squares, among men, exploring the city to its farthest corners, and the whole earth and the sky. Because everything must be as tender and warm and attractive and worthy of being known as Zilla's hand and her smile. I felt myself grow as tall as the grown-ups and then beyond them, my eyes saw further and more sharply, my breast was freed of the heavy fear which had weighed upon me since birth. It was in this moment that my mother snatched my arm and jerked me forcibly off the sofa. "Didn't you hear me?" she yelled. "Go and buy ice cream for the guests!" And she shoved me so energetically through the door that it seemed she wanted to be rid of me for good and never see me more. When the guests had gone, my mother showed her hostility still more clearly. She developed a terrible, raging headache but rejected my usual offer to stroke her brow. "Get off!" she growled, and pushed me away with her arm. I believed her to be the best and most beautiful mother in the world and was always repeating it to myself. This brusque and unloving treatment filled me with bitterness. I realized that it was all because of Erika, but I really couldn't understand why.

Next day, my mother's coldness seemed only a bad dream. We resumed our customary loving gestures, caresses and signs of affection. That she had not fully forgiven me I discovered only during the following days, when certain little, seemingly casual, accidents befell. The first occurred in the kitchen, when I was helping her to drain the pasta which replaced on Tuesdays our usual meat and vegetables. To this pasta, once cooked, was added poppyseed sweetened with sugar, or else grated walnuts. This lunch was the joy of us children and, if only to be seated quicker at table, we were prepared to help in the kitchen. "Hold the colander," said my mother, while she got busy to take the saucepan off the fire. A moment later, I felt the boiling water pour over my hands. "I told you to be careful," she scolded me in a calm voice. Fortunately, I wasn't badly scalded, and we didn't make a great fuss over it.

Three days later, another accident. We were going down the stairs. My mother had put a large package in my arms and I couldn't see properly where I was stepping. Half-way down, I heard her give a little cry of fear. Her hands fell heavily on my shoulders. I heard her shout "Help!" and down I went, the whole flight, crashing onto the landing and moaning with pain. Mother ran to help me. "Did you hurt yourself?" she asked. No, I wasn't much hurt. "We were both about to fall," she said, "I couldn't stop you in time." And she added, "I don't know what happened to me. I suddenly felt my head spinning."

The following Sunday I was on tenterhooks. Even in the morning, I seemed to see Zilla coming through the door and greeting me gaily. To please her, I also wanted to wear a white shirt. But it was missing one button at breast-height, so I asked my mother to sew it on for me. "Where did you lose it?" she demanded. I didn't know what to say. "It must have been that little hussy who pulled it off," she hissed. I didn't know whom she meant and I asked her. "That little hussy with the long plaits who you like so much," she replied in a forced, joking tone. It seemed to me that this allusion was intended as a terrible accusation. I couldn't accept it.

"Zilla isn't a hussy," I yelled. "Why do you call her a hussy?"

Mother was sitting in front of me, on a kitchen chair, and had already begun sewing on the button to the shirt I was wearing. "Why, isn't she one?" she asked, always in that same forced tone of jocularity.

"No, she isn't," I replied firmly. At that instant I felt the needle pierce my chest, right near the heart. A little prick, quite superficial.

"But why did you move?" cried my mother, beside herself. "You could have got really hurt. You're so stupid!"

She was thoroughly upset, and it took several minutes for her to calm down. I too was worked up by now, and wanted to take her to task for what she had said earlier. "Why is Zilla a hussy?" I insisted, when Mother had come to herself.

"What did you say?" she asked distractedly.

"Why did you say that Zilla is a hussy?"

"I never said so."

"Oh, yes you did."

"Let it be, my boy. Anyway, she's not coming today."

I went off to cry in secret, and when it was time to go off with my brothers for the usual morning visits, I refused. I stationed myself at the window, looking gloomily down below. Only Uncle Gustav appeared for lunch. My mother seemed very cold towards the old man, I couldn't guess

12

why. One evening of the following week, I overheard my father and mother arguing in strangled voices, something which never happened. As a rule they didn't quarrel; they kept their feelings bottled up. "You'll have to tell them!" my mother insisted, with a look she bore only in rare moments of excitement.

"You're really generous," my father sarcastically replied, "but why don't *you* tell them?"

"How do I come into it?" she asked drily. I didn't understand what they were talking about.

Then, next Sunday, I finally saw again my dear little Shadow. She arrived, as always, after lunch, coming with her mother and this time also with Emmeric. We immediately sat down side by side. "How are you?" I whispered. It was an excuse for moving still closer to her. Zilla looked at me and suddenly smiled, and I immediately sought her hand; there we were, cuddled together, paying not the slightest attention to what went on around us. Long minutes passed thus, perhaps half an hour. Once again I felt the warmth of her hand infusing me with energy and life. Then we could no longer avoid hearing the grown-ups. They were arguing furiously. My mother, Zilla's and Uncle Emmeric were all talking at once, in an agitated and wilful manner. Uncle Gustav kept silent, looking at them fixedly. "Go and have a walk," said my father; and then, turning towards my mother and speaking in a hushed voice, "Not in front of the children!"

We went down to the street. "Don't worry about us, we'll see you later, downstairs," I hastily told the eldest brother, who was charged with looking after the gang of children. And off we ran, Zilla and I, through the little

13

streets surrounding the market. She laughed even as she ran, and her plaits danced around her face. We left behind the shuttered stalls and the streets became ever more silent and peaceful. Old men were going home with packets of cakes, under scrawny, indifferent trees. Ground floor windows stood open upon dark rooms with unmade beds. We stopped only when we had no more breath and no people around us. At a corner I placed myself in front of her. I stroked her face with both hands and stood close up to her body. For the first time, I saw the smile vanish from her face, giving place to a serious and solemn expression. I buried my gaze in her eyes, so dark and shining. I had never before looked into anyone's eyes so close, so fearlessly. I seemed to have entered a world of caves and underground waters, by way of a secret passage, and to be exploring that world more in order to forget it than to know it. I felt her hand tremble slightly and her sides shake. I was drawn helplessly to her mouth, so perfectly shaped, half-open in astonishment. My face wavered around hers, my lips found her forehead, her temples, her eyes and finally her mouth in one short, tremulous kiss. We drew apart almost at once, afraid. Her eyes were darkened, but I saw as if through a veil the smile returning to her lips. We kissed again, little pecking kisses, and again and again, laughing and dancing on that street corner where by a miracle Sunday had left us alone. The kisses had become our game, invented between us, more beautiful than all the other games.

Then we began to run towards the house. I saw Zilla's legs moving fast and her blue skirt flying up to her hips as she sped along, revealing for brief moments some unknown

14

parts of her body. Then I understood that that kiss had not dissolved all the mysteries between myself and her, and that other Sundays would have enabled us to discover games and joys still richer. These were intuitions which couldn't be probed more deeply at that moment. I can do so only today, at a lifetime's distance, and with regret.

My brothers were awaiting me at the entrance, with sarcastic comments and observations barely concealing their jealousy. When we went upstairs, the grown-ups were no longer arguing. My mother's eyes were red; my father was deathly pale; my old uncle was sitting motionless at the dining table, his face buried in his hands. Emmeric and Ella were talking together, apart. Within a few minutes the guests were gone, barely bidding farewell. Zilla and I parted with a smile and a deep gaze. "Till next Sunday," I whispered, taking one of her plaits in my hand.

But there was to be no "next Sunday". "Why should we do it, when he has two children of his own?" cried my mother, in the cadence adopted by the Jews when uttering the obvious, after the front door had barely closed behind them. Her voice rose in pitch with every word, till it became quite piercing, almost a falsetto. So Uncle Gustav no longer came to take Sunday lunch with us. Let Ella and Emmeric look after him, my mother declared. Naturally, we saw no more of that pair either. And I never saw Zilla again. For me she became a soft, elusive, indistinguishable shadow which I carried in my memory all through life. What I have forgotten, burying it in the depths of my being, is the pain I suffered in having to separate myself from her. I really don't remember it, as if that pain had been fused into my soul and become one with it.

15

THE TEMPLE

The walls were bought by the Jews of the Teleky Market at the beginning of the century for the greater glory of God - and so as not to have to cross the boulevard, beyond which stood the nearest temple. The big premises of the block, half-way down Grand Transport Avenue, had until recently formed an emporium. Appropriate works of transformation and consecration had to be carried out. The windows being walled in, the offices of the Community could be located on the upper floor. And the ground floor became the temple for the merchants of the Eighth District.

This place was grand and full of mystery. When I went there for the first time, an astounding universe was opened to me, wherein the men that I saw every day haggling, arguing, toiling, appeared to me in their prayer shawls like rows of larvae streaked with black. I myself felt different there, and the space, the air, the light took on special forms and functions. I couldn't take it all in at one glance, so vast was this chamber, ranged with columns, pictures, lamps and galleries, and all crammed with worshippers. Many times I later explored this mysterious world, but always a bit at a time; now the pulpit, now the part 'down there', now that 'to the left of the entrance'; without ever being able to construct a proper map of it in my head.

The light was quite dim, and from that magical atmosphere strange apparitions would emerge, as if from nowhere. I was greatly impressed by the silvered hands which shone over the Torah, just as I was always startled and frightened by rolls of parchment pulled out from the scintillating vestments. I conceived of those whiteclad bodies as another form of life, different from our usual one (it was already 'usual', and I was only five!), with its own pulsations and customs, and a light tinkling sound, without rhythm, which couldn't be heard anywhere else.

Yes, that temple of the market Jews had something of the substance of the Temple of Heaven and of Solomon's Temple, eternal treasure of the Jewish people. How such a shining light could fall upon this spot, the belly and cesspool of Budapest, as are all the markets of all Babylons - that is the mystery of Divine Mercy. However, so it was. Every Friday I would see my father and my uncles, rapt and transfigured, bowed over their prayer books, rocking their torsos rhythmically to and fro in search of an ecstasy that never arrived. Covered in their *tales*, or prayer shawls, they would have seemed all alike if it had not been possible to gather, even there and in that moment, their essential characters: the mildness of one and the hurried seriousness of another; the stern severity of those who thought themselves better than their fellows and the overbearing sonority of those in haste to better themselves; the gloom of those without aims or desires; the fears of the old who had reached the end of their lives.

These mysteries did not awaken alarm but, rather, an unappeasable thirst for knowledge. Whilst the temple 'up there' was filled with the faithful at prayer, the one 'down below', lower by a couple of feet, formed the domain of the children, who celebrated Friday evening by chasing about and shouting, as they embarked on adventurous explorations: every brown-painted backboard was a Pillar of Hercules, and the space between two benches a continent, different from the others in its inhabitants, in the presence or absence of children, and in the length of the *tales* of those at prayer. The language spoken in the temple was quite strange to me, as it was for nearly all the children and most of the adults (knowledge of Hebrew had been lost for at least a generation), but you could distinguish various dialects. On one bench the verses would be recited with monotonous rapidity; on another, in an inarticulate murmur from which only the name of the Lord emerged distinctly; on another, with loud but punctilious clarity. I would observe each person, drawing conclusions about his character and his importance. If I met a child, I would greet him and we would explore together, up and down the temple, around the pulpit, right to the uppermost limits. Until they began to sing in unison, at the top of their voices, *"Lechò daidì, licras callà"*, "Come, friend, to meet the bride", the greeting for the coming feast-day and the closing song for Friday evening.

Occasionally, however, this fascinating and joyful world would assume an awesome face. The day of Kippur, for example, when the Torah was carried in procession through the temple, and at its passing the Jews covered their heads with their prayer shawls, my heart would be filled with terror; and also at New Year, when the *shofar*, or ram's horn, was blown, at that raucous sound, precursor of the eternal awakening in the Valley of Jehoshaphat, I would peer under my eyelids at the crowd hidden under their *tales* and feel myself far from there, among many beings already dead, who awaited a joyful resurrection. Sometimes I hadn't even the courage to look: I too tried to hide my head, burying it in my father's shawl, sure that within a moment something tremendous would occur, something beyond all my fears, the end of the world.

Then these moments would pass and the expectation of the terrible event, the arrival of the Eternal One amongst us, or of an archangel or some other representative of His, would be put off till next year.

Another fear of mine, even less explicable, was aroused by the aspect of the women's gallery, those few times we were sent there with a message for my mother or one of the aunts. This happened most frequently on the day of Kippur, when all the family was in the temple and there was sometimes a detail still to be decided about the supper. The women's gallery was very narrow, set on the upper floor and separated from the rest of the temple by a fine grille. There the women were seated, all in rows, with their faces half-covered by handkerchiefs or veils. A little pale with fasting, they seemed in that half-light as if already risen to a new life, but risen with a more severe aspect, without love, as if they had been endowed · so I felt · with the power of life and death over all children and all humanity. Once I looked down through the grille into the temple. Those below suddenly took on the look of poor ignorant insects over whom, from up there where I was at that moment, it would be easy to cast spells or curses.

Once I was back among the benches, among the children and the prayer shawls, this fear passed quickly, giving way to the peculiar, solemn joy of one who is exploring the mysteries. Because there, in the temple, apart from these moments of anxiety, the notion of evil, even if I had known its full significance, could have had no proper place. Neither the irreverences of the children, nor the reprimands whispered by the cantor between one verse and the next to these disorderly brats, had the slightest flavour of malevolence. As if my soul were armoured so as not to feel any contrary forces, prohibitions or impositions, any restraints upon my person. I had a sensation even of contentment, austere and deeply felt, which I hoped would last me through eternity.

Instead, this mysterious world was to be overturned at a stroke, that day in 1944 when we were obliged for the first time to enter the temple without the reassuring presence of our parents. One morning in late autumn my mother dressed me up, entrusted to me and my brothers a paper bag, with a few bits of bread and roast goose inside, and accompanied us as far as the door of the Community Hall. The complex discussions of the grown-ups the preceding evening had been aimed at explaining to us that we would be quite safe there, because the King of Sweden in person had bought that building and bestowed on it a special protection, so that the Germans were forbidden to cross the threshold in any circumstances, and the same applied to the local Nazis and anyone else who wanted to harm us, the children of the Jewish community. What nobody explained to us was that we would be alone, desperately alone, and for a time that no one could estimate. At the door of the hall, Mother let go our hands.

21

A skinny woman with thick glasses took us in charge, and when I turned about Mother had vanished, as if some magical force had made her invisible. "Where did she go?" I asked the community secretary, anxiously. "Don't worry, just come with me," she replied. We passed in front of the temple door, but I had time for only a glimpse of the interior; instead of going in, we continued towards the upper floor, where lay the offices of the community.

We were received in a big room whose window shutter was carefully closed. It had two doors, apart from the front one: one of them, a double door, simply led to another room like the first and the second, a single door, led into a long corridor. The double door stood open and in these two rooms, destined to be our abode for several months, we found most of the children known from the temple or from families befriended during the little parties organized by the mothers in times of peace. We had passed many hours together, but now all of us felt strange towards one another. We scarcely looked in each others' faces; there we were, thoroughly inhibited, not knowing what to expect.

Days, weeks and cruel months lay ahead of us. That evening, mattresses were spread on the floor of the two rooms and some horsehair covers thrown over them. We passed the night stretched out side by side, silently. In the morning, the community secretary took everything away and from the depths of the corridor appeared the rabbi with his assistant, to give us lessons in Scripture. Nothing of that religious instruction remains in my memory. We were in the hardest captivity that a bunch of children can expect to suffer, deprived of affection, well-being, proper food, and in our souls there was no trace of guilt or any

22

other explanation of the ills we suffered. The menaces and severity of the Good Book seemed to us injustices, tremendous injustices. Our food was distributed at midday in milk bowls: a brownish soup made with stock cubes, beans or cabbage, according to the day.

Gradually orders ceased to affect us. We gave up every habit, every rule. We no longer slept on the mattresses. Whoever felt tired just threw himself on the ground and fell asleep; whoever was hungry turned to the wall and ground his teeth. We didn't even respect any longer the regulations about our bodily needs. The latrine, accessible from the second room by a small corridor, never cleaned by anyone, was brimming with excrement. One day, tired of waiting in line, I fouled myself, standing up in my pants. I carried around this load of dung for a whole month, until the Liberation.

Not even the authority of the secretary or the rabbi counted any longer. In February 1945, while the fighting grew fiercer around us, we rebelled. We had been shut up for at least three months in the community's premises, hungry, filthy, full of fleas. It was a revolting meal which set the fuse. Our cabbage soup was full of worms. Not one of us children managed to swallow it. With empty stomach and trembling body, I burst out crying. But it was not really crying. From my throat burst bellows of protest like the roars of a bull, violent enough to shake the door and the shuttered windows. Soon my voice was joined by those of my brothers and all the other children. "I'm hungry!" cried one of them. Many others copied my complaints and began beating their fists on the wooden floor of the rooms. Ludwig Grosz, now a doctor in America, tore the clothes off

23

his back; the bespectacled Maurer pissed on the floor; some children began vomiting gobs of stinking gall. Then, like the exterminating angel, the rabbi appeared in the depths of the corridor. He smothered our hysterical cries with one stentorian shout. Swinging one arm, he knocked a bunch of children to the floor; eyes flaming and body crouched, he burst among us, ready to knock us down or break us in two. "If he's so strong, it means he hasn't been eating worm-infected cabbage, but something better," I thought. And perhaps I even said it, because a moment later I felt myself swept away as if by a gust of wind, an explosion of energy hit me in the cheek and I fell unconscious to the ground. I spent many days like that, stretched out and void of strength. When I came to myself, I learned of the end of the revolt from the faces of the other children, all pale, disconsolate and deprived of any flicker of vitality. The only concession we won was the abolition of cabbage. As I remember it, from then on we were given nothing but beans.

It was still winter when we finally left our prison and place of refuge. We had endured day after day of a real witches' sabbath. The time came when the rooms of the community were lacking even electric light. The hanging lamps which had lit our rooms now dangled useless from the ceiling; just two strips of daylight filtered through the blinds to give us a small field of vision. Even the water was now cut off, and for three days and nights we heard the cannonade drawing ever closer, shaking the walls of our rooms. This was the first time that I saw fear in the eyes of the rabbi, until the moment of decision arrived. "We must send them away from here," he said, not to us but to the secretary. "It's both just and advisable." Soon after this exchange, we children were thrust into the overcoats abandoned on our arrival and conducted downstairs. We were taken outside in groups. As for me, I was one of the last. I stopped dead at the door of the temple. It was the first time for ages that I saw the light of day. I lifted my eyes. Two planes were fighting in the grey sky overhead. I saw red tracers speeding from one plane towards the other: two battling angels soared in a sky immersed in the thunder of bombardment. Then, in an instant, the two angels disappeared behind the roof of the temple, still exchanging their red arrows of gunfire. And a moment later an unspeakable thunder shook us and all the buildings around. The bomb had fallen quite nearby. The spectacled Maurer and many more of my companions of those months were carried off by the Angel of Death in that terrible explosion. I still ask myself why.

But I didn't even expect answers to anything when I again visited the temple and the community, many years later. I told myself that the universe is growing old and we will need other worlds, not this one, to find again the joy we knew when we were children.

It was absent-minded wandering which carried my steps into that street. Lifting my eyes to the peeling façade, I saw written in Hebrew: *Bet Keneset,* the meeting house or synagogue. I crossed over. The low doorway was not as I remembered it. I pushed open the swinging doors easily but had great difficulty in finding the right passage. When I was finally in the temple, I felt my throat contract. The inscrutable architecture of many years before had disappeared, as if the shrinking of the Jewish population of the district had even decimated the brickwork and the tiles. The place of sacred gatherings was now cramped, faded and wretched. Where were the columns? I could see only two supports thrown up in the middle of the chamber. And the benches? Many were broken, and almost all had large areas of paint missing, which exposed their real construction in a greyish and riddled wood. Only the railings of the pulpit had been polished, along with the ante-room to the tabernacle. The floor consisted of broken or cracked bricks, and on the walls dust had darkened the whitewash. This looks more like a witches' coven than the temple of the Lord, I thought. Here was no lodging for joy; here only misery presided, and it had sunk its teeth deep into the place.

I went up to a bench and put my hands on it. For a moment, it was as though a sudden light had driven the darkness from my eyes. I saw a flock of Jews rocking themselves and murmuring their prayers; the space stretched out into the far distance, and the bells of the Torah could be heard softly tinkling. The Jews were covered in their *tales* up to the tops of their heads and white clothing was visible beneath them. "Come and pray with us," I heard someone whisper. I shuddered, because that voice could not be disobeyed, the call of the dead being sacred and fatal.

A tremor passed over me and darkened my sight once more. The praying flock vanished, but an old man was coming up behind me. I gave another start and jumped backwards. "Are you looking for something?" he asked me, taking at the same time imperceptible steps towards me. I scrutinized him and felt my eyes fill with tears. I soon recognized Samuel Stern, the cantor of long ago. His face was shrunken and the eyes seemed veiled. "Are you looking for something?" he repeated.

"Uncle Stern, how are you? I'm one of your old pupils," I murmured. It was he who had taught me to read Hebrew. But Stern continued to gaze at me interrogatively. "I came just to visit the temple!" I shouted, to overcome his deafness and suspicion.

"Ah, there's nobody here," was his sole reply, "few people come now. Most of them died, during the war." I shouted again that as a child I too had frequented that temple; he just stood there perplexed. For Samuel Stern the living no longer existed, only the dead. Perhaps it was my voice: for a large piece of old stucco fell from the ceiling, breaking into dust at our feet. I was startled, but the old man didn't bat an eyelid. "The limewash..." he said. I stroked his cheek with a caress before departing. I wanted to go up to the community's rooms, to see again the place of my childhood sufferings. But the staircase was no longer there. I could see only a walled-up niche. Once in the street, the enigma was solved. The upper floor now had a separate entrance and housed a state company. For me, all things considered, it was a relief not being able to enter that room of long ago. I should have met myself as a child, and that child would have demanded what I had done with the rest of my life. "I saved myself," he would have asserted, "and you, what have you done with the stolen years?"

THE SEVEN LOVERS

I went to the cinema, for distraction, after many wretched days. They were showing some old American movie, a dramatic and far-fetched love story. "Music by Miklòs Brodsky" flashed up on the screen. Meanwhile, the soundtrack was already playing a sweet, romantic piece of piano music, the notes of an old song that I'd heard as a child. The words of the chorus I still knew by heart:

I have no sweet memories of you,
You only made me suffer
So many hours of weeping, so many lost nights
Begging in the rain for your love.

I recalled that Brodsky too had been one of the Jews of the Eighth District of Budapest, before going off to Hollywood, and that I knew the words of the song so well because it had been written for someone who had sung it to me many times: Ilona Weiss, the belle of our quarter many years ago, now an old lady whose hair was burnt with dyeing and whose legs were all shrivelled up, but who still sang occasionally, suffocating her nostalgia by puffing cheap cigarettes. She had once been like that music, lovely, tender, ephemeral. And for all the love she had excited, she was left with nothing but a handful of banknotes.

She had come to Budapest when scarcely an adolescent, from some village near the Russian border. Two older sisters had brought her up and helped her to blossom. One took her into the house and gave her her own daughter for company. The other sewed her new clothes as she outgrew the old, or as soon as they went out of fashion. She didn't skimp on materials, and the designs were the latest that she, sister Erna, had seen around town on the backs of rich young women, the styles just in from Vienna or Paris. Erna copied them to perfection, because she had real hands of gold when it came to cutting or sewing.

And so this girl with the big nut-brown eyes grew up. She studied little and badly, preferring to hang about town or visit the cafés with her friends. The boys of the quarter all admired her. She played them along and then humiliated them - a game she learned early on and never forgot. In her shining black hair she wore clasps and ribbons. Her legs were well turned and her waist slender. At sixteen she grew large, firm breasts whose nipples were darkly ringed, like flowers.

At seventeen she was already renowned for her gaiety; she knew by heart all the songs then in vogue.

At eighteen she began looking forward with excitement and some trepidation to the debutantes' ball for young Jewesses. Erna made her an outfit which was extraordinarily becoming: a red blouse of pure silk and a pleated skirt fringed with lace. She thrust a blushing rose in her hair.

"You, come and dance," said Miko Kelemen, eldest son

of a jeweller. The Kelemens had changed their name some time earlier, at the beginning of the century, when the birth of the national state was swelling all bosoms with patriotic emotion. And then the Kelemens - or the Kohns, if you want to be nasty about it - strove not to remember their Jewish origins at any price. Their customers were the best families in the country. For these counts and barons they obtained fine bracelets and Venetian goldwork, exquisite glass and mirrors from Murano, English silver cutlery of extraordinary workmanship. But at the same time, they didn't altogether renounce an honourable role even in the Jewish community. Ida, Miko's mother, went to the temple for all the festivals and wanted good Jewish girls for all her sons; there were two other boys, Ernest and Andrew, apart from Miko.

Every year, the family coughed up a large donation for the community, of which the father served as a councillor. Their apartment lay near the National Theatre, still within the Eighth District but in a very elegant street, and there they entertained many young Jews, both boys and girls, for discussions of culture and politics. Some of these wrote poetry, some of the boys attended the university, all were comfortably off.

The wild girl with the rose in her hair and the jeweller's son danced together all evening. Miko was proud to have chosen the prettiest and most provocative debutante of the occasion. Sweating and laughing, red in the face, he tried in vain to read her expression. He could not penetrate Ila's deep look; the girl was rejecting this first, innocent but dangerous proposal of love. "Shall we meet tomorrow at the Hungaria?" he whispered, late that night, when the party

31

was almost over. And Ila, who all evening had concentrated her attention on the songs, repeating their words quietly while she danced, clasping Miko, but far away from him in her thoughts, smiled at him for the first time. "As you wish," she replied. She didn't want people to make unpleasant remarks about her ambition, nor to appear to be a gold-digger. If he wanted to see her so desperately, that was his affair. Saying yes to such a request didn't signify that she was picking forbidden fruit. It signified simply that she said yes, with no other implications.

That Miko was a fairly forbidden fruit, Ila, the immigrant from the Russian borderlands, knew well enough. Even this appointment at the Hungaria Café was rather suspect. The Hungaria was not far from the Café Emke, frequented by Jews of little account - not more than five hundred yards along the street. But in the social scale the distance was enormous, not to be counted in yards but in ringing coins. The Hungaria was the haunt of many noblemen, patriotic poets and rich Jews. Not of the sons and daughters of small tradesmen.

"Did Miko like you?" demanded the indiscreet Erna on the way home.

"I can't say," replied the girl, pulling the rose from her hair.

"How do you mean, you can't say? Didn't he ask to see you again?" Erna insisted.

"But what's got into you?" retorted Ila. Years later, when she herself told me the story, I asked her why she had fibbed. "It was my affair whether I saw Miko again or not. I didn't want other people getting mixed up in it," was her explanation.

Miko was wildly in love with Ila. After that appointment at the Hungaria, he treated her to all the most elegant cafés in the city, the most renowned ballrooms, and exclusive restaurants in Buda, where girls of the Eighth District never set foot. He followed like a faithful dog when Ila went walking with her friends, with his eyes fixed on her, begging just for a look. He seized her hand, when Ila let him have it for a few moments, and squeezed it as if it had been that of his guardian angel, his last hope of salvation. But Ila gave him nothing more. Until the day came when Miko carried her by car through all the most beautiful and select streets of the city, the most silent quarters. "Ila, I must say good-bye," he said suddenly, after a long interval. "I've got to go away." He turned towards her with shining eyes. "My mother is sending me away. She says I must forget you. But I'll never forget you, never!" He tried to embrace her, whispering brokenly, "Give me a farewell kiss."

But she pushed him off, snapping, "If your mother says you must forget me, forget me!"

Miko left for Paris. For two years Ila heard nothing more of the Kelemens. But one day Miko's brother Ernest came to look for her. "Come, I beg you. Miko wants to see you for the last time." The young man had returned from Paris a few weeks earlier, completely drained of blood. Tuberculosis had emptied his veins. Ila did not refuse. This was the first time she had set foot in the house of the jeweller Kelemen. She greeted no one. They conducted her straight to the bedside of the dying lover. Miko's eyes were shining and his cheeks aflame, just as when he had courted her so timidly and passionately. When he saw the

33

girl, he summoned up a smile and wearily offered her his left hand. Ila didn't take it; after a moment she looked away and left the room. He died that same evening.

"He couldn't die without seeing you," said Andrew, the youngest brother, after the funeral.

"Scarcely six months later," Ila told me once, "the elder of the two brothers phoned me and said he wanted to talk to me." He had already married before Miko's death, and his father had opened a small jeweller's for him, right in the centre of the city. "He was alone when I went to see him, just before closing time. He bent over the counter, all red in the face, and spluttered in one breath that he knew what wrongs his parents had done me, and what wrong I had done to his brother, but that he wanted me so much, more than anything else in the world, that his marriage was a disaster, that his wife was a nasty woman who didn't even know how to build a happy home full of love and that he had desperate need of a girl full of life like me and was ready to give me anything whatsoever."

"And how did you reply?"

"I slapped him. I asked him if he took me for a whore or a kept woman. I said that no one could lay anything to my account; if he needed happiness he should go and tickle up his wife." Ernest had turned from bright red to as white as a sheet, burbling some words of excuse and a renewed invitation to "become friends", while Ila was already storming out of the shop. "He imagined he could buy me with a string of pearls. But he made a big mistake," snorted Ila, all those years later. She didn't speak with contempt, but rather with commiseration, for a sad fate hung over Ernest. He was found one evening with

34

a revolver bullet in his head. He had shot himself.

"Because of me? No, I'd nothing to do with it," said Ila, with her eyes fixed vacantly. "He was the wild one, who wasn't content with his own wife. No one dared put the blame on me. Anyway, what could I have done?"

And the third brother? He too would have been glad to cull that great dark flower which was Ila, to kiss her lips, hold her burning breasts. Ila talked with him a few evenings after that scene in the brother's jewellery shop.

Andrew was the best looking and most lively of the three, the most sincere. "I promise you nothing. Only a mouth that knows how to kiss," he cried jokingly, suddenly seizing her by the waist. The girl waited a moment before freeing herself. Then she said, "Go to the devil, you too." She saw him again only at his marriage. A registry office marriage, with no religious ceremony, because Andrew was marrying a *schikse,* the Christian daughter of one of the family's domestic servants. A pretty blonde girl, with an expressionless face which in a few years, Ila reflected, would fade. For that reason alone, Ila was satisfied. She went to the City Hall to see and to talk. Not to Andrew, but to the mother, Mrs Kelemen, who hadn't wanted her as a daughter-in-law.

"You wouldn't give your sons to me. Now you're happy that the youngest is being taken by a Christian skivvy," she said. They were in the street, in front of the City Hall. The old woman stood there petrified and Ila went off without waiting for a reply.

"And afterwards, what happened?"

"I've never been a whore, I've never taken money from anyone, even if I was a poor Jew," Ila exclaimed.

35

The fourth lover was a wine merchant. He had seen Ila in the temple and spoke to a marriage broker. He was plump, middle-aged, and dressed like a bumpkin. Ila despised him from the first moment. She agreed to meet him, to sip coffee with him, to meet him again and put up with his rapt gaze fixed on her breasts. Only then did she ask him bluntly, "What do you want of me?" The man babbled that he only wanted to make her happy. "Make me happy? How might that be?" she demanded scornfully.

"I can make you happy," he replied. "If you marry me, I shan't let you want for anything, and I'll look after your sisters too. You can even buy your clothes in Paris."

This was just what Ila was waiting for. She screwed up her eyes and hissed like a snake. She exclaimed that she wasn't a whore, that she didn't sell herself for fourpence to the first lecherous old man who came along, and that she wouldn't put up with any further molestation. As for him, he shouted that he could find plenty of girls in his own village and drown them all in wine. Then she swept off, leaving the wine merchant in the middle of the Café Emke. "I did it all by instinct, but I was right," she claimed. "Soon after that he took to drink and destroyed himself. A drunken Jew is a scourge."

The fifth lover looked like having more luck. Bèla Weiss was a bold fellow, the son of a railway porter. He would never humiliate himself before her. They got married. He was a taxi driver and his father found clients for him. In that way, Bèla could make a little bit extra, but not much.

"That friend of yours, the musician, didn't you like him?"

"Of course I liked him. He had eyes and hair as black

as coal. He was always elegant, always perfumed."

"Why didn't you marry him?"

"Brodsky had nothing in his head but success, Hollywood, the big scene. However, one day he came back from America, met up with me and said, 'Ila, tonight I'll play only for you.' We went into a café and he sat down at the piano, with me leaning nearby. We stayed there till dawn, he playing and I singing. The people around us listened in amazement. For the last song, we gave *I have no sweet memories of you*. Then we said good-bye. Just 'Ciao, Ila!' I never saw him again."

Every time she told me that story, Ila would sing this famous song again, from beginning to end. Perhaps she wasn't in love with Brodsky, but with his songs she certainly was. And Bèla Weiss? I don't know. Their marriage was not blessed with children; the beautiful Ila was sterile. Bèla was addicted to gambling. He would spend hours in the café playing cards, and often he lost the day's earnings. Ila was always arguing with him about it. Until the great Holocaust put an end to all such quarrels.

Bèla sleeps in a common grave at Auschwitz. He was still alive at the end of the war, though reduced to a skeleton. By means of a fellow prisoner more fortunate than himself, he sent greetings to Ila. "Tell her I'm really not up to coming home, that I send her a kiss."

Ila had escaped extermination by hiding in Budapest. During a raid by the Germans, she was caught in a cellar. "Shoot me here, if you like!" she cried, baring her breasts. The soldier didn't have the heart to bloody such fine petalled flowers. Or so she recounted it, priding herself more on her courage than on her beauty.

37

The sixth lover was a simple artisan, a tailor from the provinces, Alex Klein, neither handsome nor bold. A sickly creature. In the Holocaust he had lost his wife and his two sons, real jewels of children. Ila, inexplicably, agreed to be his consolation. At forty she was still provocative, rather than beautiful. I never saw her touch or embrace Alex, nor any other man. Perhaps it was just for this reason that she had married Klein; she was sure that this man wouldn't bother her much, or for long.

What she wouldn't accept from the wine merchant, Ila accepted from the tailor. Klein allowed her to lack nothing. He bought her the finest clothes and perfumes. In their apartment near the People's Theatre one didn't notice that paucity of furnishings which characterized almost all the apartments in the district. Carpets, china ornaments and armchairs filled the sitting room; the bathroom was fitted with mirrors and a modern water heater. What is more, from her wedding day onwards, Ila was able to cast off her goose-seller's apron and stay at home doing nothing. The porter's wife took care of the cleaning of the apartment. All that remained for her to do was to prepare some sweets made with poppyseed or milk curds, for Saturdays and Sundays.

Alex was able to give her all this, thanks to a little shop on the main road, one of the few workshops not swept up by state ownership. Only a few square yards of floor space and one miserable window. He had bought it from an old acquaintance with the war compensation money he received from Germany. A pretty bitter consolation for one who had lost his wife and beloved children. But one has to go on living.

38

Alex sewed nothing but skirts. In the morning he received customers, in the afternoon he scoured the town for materials, and in the evening he sat himself down at the sewing table squeezed into the narrow space behind the shop. Returning to the house, he would pick a book at random from the bookcase in the sitting room - a tiny library, but perhaps unique among so many traders' houses - and read a few pages. Then he said good-bye to the day with a long fit of coughing.

Of life itself he understood nothing. He never understood why his family had been wiped out; nor why he, cowardly and fearful as he was, had managed to survive; nor why that little shop had brought him so much money when all around him, formerly rich merchants and industrialists could barely scrape a living. He never understood why he, a little upside-down Job, after God had taken everything from him, was now inundated with blessings: an abundant income and that wife, so beautiful, cheerful, the envy of everyone. To distract himself a little from the unsolvable enigmas of his own life, he would philosophize over the enigmas of the world: the Cold War, America, Russia, the future political order of the planet. "Where shall we end up?" he was still asking when I last visited him in the hospital.

It was the cough that carried him off, after twenty years of marriage. Ila bought him a comfortable plot in the Jewish cemetery, right near the entrance. In truth, the comfort was for herself, for poor Alex could have slept equally well anywhere. But in this way Ila, when still scarcely out of the tram, would have almost reached his tomb, to leave behind at every visit two little tears, one for

39

each eye, and a pebble dropped on the grave, according to Jewish custom. She bought that tomb for eight thousand florins. She had a good few thousands left to live on, enough to last easily for several years. Only after ten years had passed since her husband's death did she begin to worry a little, and to ask herself if it might be wise to marry for the third time. She told herself no, and said no also to Dr Schreiber, the broker of the community, when he proposed to her "a good match".

So ended the loves of Ila, the most beautiful woman of our quarter. Even in old age, she hasn't renounced her looks. Always elegant and striking in her dress. Every Wednesday evening she has a meeting with some friends of her youth. She brings an apple cake, others chocolate, fruit or some sweet liqueur. Then they all begin to sing, and when it's time for the song *I have no sweet memories of you,* Ila always has tears in her eyes. Cigarettes have made her voice hoarse. Her legs have grown skinny; her breasts have fallen.

One evening, when returning from the weekly gathering in the block of flats where her friends live, Ila encountered an unfamiliar neighbour. "Like to come with me?" said this unknown admirer to her, as they went downstairs. Or perhaps she only thought she had heard it.

"I reached the doorway with my heart in my mouth. I had a terrible throbbing in my temples," she recounted. She is afraid of the seventh lover. Every week she touches up her hair with a pale red dye. She wants to be more beautiful than ever when the hour comes for the last embrace. The one not even she can refuse.

FRANJA THE FOX

The last time I visited the old Jewish cemetery in Kozma Street was two years ago. I went there expressly to look for the tomb of one of my distant relatives; something I had failed to do hitherto. But one night, who knows why, I found myself thinking of her, Franja Leuchtner, and of her tomb on which, perhaps ever since she died, no one had placed a pebble. A few days later I jumped into my car; I crossed mountains, rivers, frontiers, just to discharge my duty. What happened during my pious visit still unsettles me today. I shall never return to that cemetery. I haven't the strength for it.

But before telling you about my experience, terrifying as it was, to help you understand better the significance of what occurred, I must talk about Franja herself, one of my great aunts or something of the kind. A distant relative, whose existence I knew of more from the accounts of other relatives than from direct knowledge, and whom - while she was alive - I visited seldom and liked still less.

She had come to the capital from a small village in Slovakia before the First World War; at that time she must have been about nine or ten. She and her sister Lilli, together with their father, who was soon left a widower, opened a small tavern on the edge of the city. The older sister cooked - by all accounts, she was an exceptional cook - and Franja served the customers, who were mostly of the suburban working class. These, when they lifted their elbows, which was almost every evening, were not sparing in their ribaldry even with her, not yet an adolescent.

The father, who was strongly built and of regal deportment, but with the heart of a lamb, didn't dare to interfere. What's more, these *rosche* - that is, people who dislike Jews - were of the worst sort, and despised the three tavern-keepers for their origin; so it would have taken more than a little boldness to check their disposition and heavy irony. When a customer, at the peak of his drunken delirium, staggered off breathing oaths against "these dirty Jews", the old man was so content to see him go without causing further damage, that he never considered asking him to settle up. Run in this fashion, the tavern soon turned a loss. The three persevered, in toil and misery, until the end of the war. The day when the old man closed the shutters of his tavern for the last time, he cried, "*Glaübt zi Gott!* Thank God, this nightmare is over!" Franja, on the other hand, who had now grown into a buxom and pretty girl (*molette,* or plump, her father said), was a little downcast. Unknown to her father, she had put away a nice little nest egg, between tips, sleights of hand and short measures poured to copious drinkers. Nor had she hesitated to accept the odd pinch of her bottom or breasts, or to give the odd kiss, just to keep these drunkards happy. Apart from this, she wasn't a very bright girl, and she would respond to either compliments or heavy slaps with the slightly vacant smile of one who doesn't

42

comprehend the yet heavier meaning of these words and actions.

She had the reputation of being a bit slow. When she was a little girl in Slovakia, a cock had attacked her and nearly punctured her skull with ferocious pecks. By the time the father had come to her rescue, she was already senseless on the ground. The slow and careful manner, the slanting gaze, the foolish smiles of Franja, which she preserved to the end of her days, were perhaps due to this accident. But God had granted her, maybe in compensation for these ills, a quite exceptional astuteness.

The Torah was, in truth, still written upon the very bodies of the Chosen People, as my old religious teachers insisted, if the importance which God gave to a miserable life like Franja's was so great. Only someone who manages to read the whole meaning of this living book, a great *hohem*, or sage, will be able to comprehend that. But where do we find such a mind today? Certainly not in me, who am capable only of trembling before cases so tragic as the one I'm about to describe.

But to return to Franja, towards the middle of the 'twenties she was presented with a possible match to a Polish shoemaker, who worked with half a dozen others in a small but well-established workshop. The young man was educated and good-looking, and had hopes of making rapid progress in the firm. Franja's father was no less satisfied than the daughter who, however, for some strange reason, soon began to display a certain reluctance. The real motive revealed itself only two or three years later, and in a dramatic fashion. Until this moment she certainly could not have confessed to her father that during the Sunday afternoon promenades and the visits to the Café Emke, much frequented by Eighth District Jews of small to middling income, they had exchanged a few little kisses. In those brief moments she, with her acute sense of smell, had detected a strange odour, of camphor or of phenol - of the hospital, in short. "I am a fox in these matters," Franja said of herself, "I can smell everything." And so it proved. After an interminable two-year engagement, the young man came one evening to Franja's house, and that very night his destiny was accomplished. Turning up with cakes and candies at the home of his consenting fiancée, he was seized in the midst of a happy conversation about future arrangements by a terrible fit of coughing, until a huge gob of blood burst from his throat onto the table, which was already prepared for supper. The boy, who had kept his consumption hidden throughout the engagement, died within three weeks - may he rest in God - almost on the eve of his intended wedding. At the sight of so much blood and in the proximity of death, Franja said simply: "You see? I suspected it. I'm a fox." From that day onwards, "Fox" became her nickname.

Some three years after the fiancé's death, I think, she married his immediate boss, a sort of foreman of the workers. He too was a Pole and a cobbler, Karl Leuchtner by name.

Frances, as Franja was really called, left her father's house and moved to a little one-room apartment on the first floor of the building with railings which stands right on the corner of Matyas Square and Danko Street. Like a good Jewess, she cut her hair short and began wearing the *schejtel* type of wig, and for some time she also left off

44

work, for she became pregnant right away. The Almighty showed her no mercy; Franja the Fox gave birth to a son who had to be operated on the first day of his life, due to a serious malformation of the brain.

The hospital doctor, a *rosche*, said it would have been much better if the creature had never come into the world, but Franja, weeping and yelling, kicked up such a fuss that the words were withdrawn, leaving the Leuchtner couple a little room for hope. Karl the cobbler, small in stature and with features incredibly like Hitler's, was not convinced, however. A few months later he told his wife that he must leave for Brussels (then a remote corner of the globe for a Jew of the Eighth District), with a view to a better job and higher pay. So off he went, and Franja let him go, well knowing that she might never see him more. To this slightly obtuse woman it seemed preferable to bring up an unhappy son alone than to have the added struggle with a desperate husband; he, however, after about two years, did return to Franja the Fox and the child, who in the meantime had grown up healthy and intelligent, just as if the operation had made him completely normal. Karl came back because he had heard, by word passed from friend to friend all the way to Brussels, that Franja had become a real *oischer*, a rich woman. He, meanwhile, had achieved nothing in Brussels, and no one understood what had induced him to go there.

How had this come about? He had left her desperate and distracted. And Franja really was so, to the point of conceiving the terrible notion of suicide in her slow mind, but a little word had sufficed to open up to her amazing shrewdness the spark of hope. This was written · and

45

everything else, much more terrible, regarding Franja - in the book of destiny.

One day, when she went with her child to take a little sun in Matyas Square, three Gypsy boys stopped nearby, paying her compliments which were half flattering and half injurious. She began talking to them. They were three jockeys from the race track. Three poor fellows without arts or parts. A plan began to burgeon in her mind, a divine spark, perhaps a fragment of the omnipresent *shekinah*, God abiding among His people.

She invited them to lunch next day, then hurried off to her sister's and asked her to cook all the most succulent dishes that the Jewish cuisine of the Eighth District could conceive of: the cabbage-and-pasta soup called *Grenadier-marsch,* boiled goose, cabbage strudel, grated pumpkin and so forth.

For two months she entertained those three poor devils every day, and they couldn't believe their luck. As jockeys they became a little too heavy, but as men, one might say, they could touch the sky with one finger. Never in their lives had they imagined they could one day be so glutted. But then, without their realizing it, came the day for expressing their gratitude. Franja, with a gentle lack of interest, began asking which of the horses running that day had won. The three understood that Franja didn't expect simple information from them, but a real proof of their friendship. So as not to bid good-bye to those delicious lunches, they gave her the names of the winning horses for the next Saturday afternoon.

Franja had never lifted a finger if she could help it, not even to switch off the light! Not so her sister. And in fact

Franja sent her, Lilli, to back these names at the race track. Lilli, poor thing, didn't even know what a race track was, or that one could put money on horses, but her fiancé certainly did, only too well! And that's why Franja stated one condition: "All the winnings must be mine. Otherwise, you're capable of betting again and losing everything. No! No one will do that to me!" On Saturday evening, Lilli and her fiancé returned to Franja and poured onto the table more money than perhaps anyone in the Eighth District had ever seen at one time. Franja's fortune was made. With a subtly diminished entertainment of her jockeys, to whom she even denied ever having bet at all, she consulted her father and Lilli about what they should do with the winnings. Franja had no real profession of her own. But some way had to be found to invest the money without too much risk. Who knows why Franja's choice fell on the purchase of a stall in the Teleky Square Market? The merchandise to be bought and sold consisted of geese and other poultry. The purchasers were the lower middle class *goyte* of the quarter and the working class from the Land of the Angels area.

Before putting on the big apron of waxed canvas typical of the goose-seller, Franja yearned to satisfy one of her caprices. She went to a highly elegant furrier in Vaci Street and bought a beautiful silver-blue fox fur, which would be the envy not only of the small-time Jews of the Eighth District, but perhaps even of a countess or a princess. A fox! What strange current from the soul had awoken in Franja this particular desire? Or was it simply fate? I don't know, will never know. Anyway, Franja went with this fox fur to the Café Emke and got the Gypsies to sing, *I went*

47

to the market with Fanny Schneider, listening with her face quite bright with pleasure, while her deficient son beat the time with clumsy hands. Some time now passed. Karl Leuchtner, as I've already said, came back to his wife, who readmitted him to the house as easily as she had let him go. As for the boy, he was now being taught in a school for handicapped children. He grew up burdened with the knowledge that he might suddenly change for the worse, from one moment to the next.

And bad luck, as it always does, gradually poisoned the too-good fortune that the Almighty had poured out in such full measure for Franja the Fox. Good and evil always walk together, like twin brothers who move inseparably until the Day of the Messiah, and even then, perhaps, they will remain united. Franja made heaps of money from her stall, but of what value was it when her son began to develop strange contortions, a permanent grimace, and sudden epileptic fits which threw him to the ground? Meanwhile, in the Eighth District, the words "dirty Jew" resounded with ever greater frequency and boldness, until they became enraged shouts, accompanied by blows, confiscations, spits and insults.

Franja the Fox, with the help of her husband, sewed up all her money, which wasn't negligible, in three overcoats, one for each member of the family. The same coats on which, a few months later, they were obliged by the security regulations to sew the infamous (in the eyes of the *rosche*) Mogen David, the yellow taffeta star. The bloodbath which ensued, the real Satanic festival, drew the unfortunate shoemaker into the throat of death. The Angel got him in a forest in the Ukraine, where Karl Leuchtner

48

was seen for the last time, fastened by ice to a bare tree, frozen like an animal.

But the Most High saved Franja the Fox - though not her money - and by a miracle her son also, now grown into a man, if we adhere precisely to the idiom. There was a plan in the life and in the death of Franja, and everything was established to contribute to its fulfilment.

After the war life started up again in the Eighth District. First with a petty black market: with a few ounces of flour - mostly mixed with plaster - with flint stones, saccharine and lard. Then Franja and the other survivors re-established contact with the peasants, getting hold of fresh eggs, a little milk, a few chickens, then hens, then geese, and finally the stalls reopened their shutters and the old ice-boxes were once more filled with artificial ice. The blessing of the Lord again showered upon those little wooden stalls, bringing money with it. But how long could it last? Three years, seven, ten at most. The new political order, the new regime, soon pushed the packets of banknotes and jewels back into the mattresses and the linings of coats. The new calamity (for these petty traders) came like a final blow. "But what's this? To be deprived of our own property? What does it mean? Only God can give or take away. Working for others, at the least mistake, at the least little speculation, to be dragged off to prison like some thief?" How many times, as a child, have I heard such words! But there was worse to come. Even going to the temple on Fridays could be construed as a source of suspicion. Anyone, perhaps just to revenge himself for some loss suffered seven or eight years earlier, during the war, could accuse anyone else, in safety and anonymity, of

49

any crime whatever. For Franja this was intolerable; not even to know the name of one's enemy. "The name of God is hidden, but that of a *rosche,* who wants to send you to prison just for the hell of it, no, that can't be! It would be an obscenity! Evil must have a name!"

Franja withdrew from business together with Lilli, her partner (their father having died before the war), and went to live in a two-room house in Erdeli Street, devoting herself to her son, ever more deformed and now suddenly unable even to tell one person from another. When he died, Franja bought a tomb in the old Jewish cemetery in Kozma Street, and she bought it for two. Some time later, in fact, she also died, after fearful solitude and a prolonged, threatening disturbance of the mitral valve of the heart. Franja's last request was to be buried along with her precious fox fur, miraculously saved from the war, the confiscations, the upheavals, but now completely out of fashion and probably almost worthless. But it is now that the real mystery begins.

A few months before her death, I went to see Franja. She was withered and bent, with bluish cheeks. Nothing remained of the pretty girl of the photographs, of Franja the Fox with the obtuse but exciting glance; she had become a shadow. She kept repeating her son's name and smiling. When I was leaving, she asked me for a kiss. I hesitated. She shook her head, as if to say, "Refuse a kiss to a poor old woman on her own, with one foot in the grave? Why?" Above all in our family, and one might say in the Eighth District generally, these innocent but genuine carnal contacts signified life itself, and were practised to the utmost, at every moment of the day. To deny her a kiss

50

was like denying her life itself. I never saw her again. Her money was left to Lilli, still alive and kicking. I was in fact with her, with Aunt Lilli, when the terrifying miracle at the cemetery befell. One night Franja the Fox had appeared to me when I was dozing; well nourished, happy and serene. She gave me an inviting smile. I felt an excess of remorse; I had never visited her tomb. I set off for Budapest, I won't say just to do this, but almost. I looked up Lilli, delighted her with a ride in my car, and fixed a day to visit the Jewish cemetery. At the entrance we came upon two or three armed men. What were they doing there? A fine-looking Gypsy, who was looking after the tombs, saw the number plate of my car and asked if I had any dollars to exchange. I had the money, a ten-dollar bill, and as she was giving me the change - much more than the official rate - she warned us to be careful. There were wild animals around the place. We laughed. It was just her joke, to distract us from too close an examination of her activities.

When we got to Franja's tomb, which lay far from the entrance, among rows of dusty green trees and rough undergrowth, we stopped. Aunt Lilli cried a little, then tapped on the paving stone with a pebble. There followed a loud, raucous cry and from a large hole in the tomb, which Jews sometimes leave "for the exit of the soul", burst a fox, yes, really a fox! that hurtled against me with terrible force. I just had time to see his fiery eyes, his sharp fangs, and to smell the infernal stench of his breath. Then with a fist, by sheer instinct, I hit out at him. I began kicking at the furious beast, which wanted to bite me at all costs. The battle lasted perhaps a minute, a minute and a half, and then, with his mouth all bloody, the brute ran back into

51

the tomb, disappearing in a flash.

Aunt Lilli was stretched on the ground, swooning. I took her in my arms and hastened away with her, turning every few moments like a man pursued. The three armed men came towards us, three hunters. I didn't look where they went. I put the old woman into the car and rushed off. Never again have I visited that cemetery, nor my few surviving relatives, nor my native city. A few months later I got a letter from my third cousin, who wrote: "The poor Jewish cemetery has fallen into the utmost neglect. Wild animals have begun to make their lairs in the tombs."

But these events, like Franja's whole existence, open the eyes towards mysteries far deeper and of far greater import than such an ingenuous comment can even glimpse.

THE TABLES OF THE LAW
OF SELMA GRÜN

"We must live in obscurity" was the chief maxim of Selma
Grün, stamped, as it were, on her whole existence, and on
that of her numerous relations. Three generations later, her
descendants still carried this obscurity with them like a
curse. They avoided people, walked with their eyes on the
ground, lived in dark houses in which their imaginations
conjured up sad events and painful deaths. The passage in
the Scriptures where it is written, "People of Israel, shut
yourselves in your houses!" was not really about this at all.
But Selma knew little of the Scriptures, and after a certain
point didn't want to know them better.

She was a woman of enormous girth, renowned among
the goose-dealers of the Eighth District and the Gypsies -
almost all of them porters or musicians - for her
prodigality, which bordered on recklessness, but also for
her terrible fits of anger. Modesty was, therefore, the last
thing you would associate with Selma Grün. Nevertheless,
she had been preaching it ceaselessly for decades, even
imposing it on those who accepted her domination: that is
to say, her two younger brothers, her three sisters, her
daughter, and her acquired relations, the neighbours.
Selma had the soul of a queen. Her kingdom was the

market in Teleky Square, over which she had imposed, throughout her life, the law of obscurity.

Nobody remembered just when she had appeared in the Eighth District. It was known that she came from the province of Nytra in Slovakia, and that she had come along with her father, recently bereaved and with all those children to look after. What had moved him to give up his birthplace, where he had been reasonably prosperous, no one had ever understood. Perhaps a dream, a nocturnal vision; how many empires have been born in that way! The great Empire was, moreover, the place for every kind of dreaming, but there was no means of waking from it.

It happened that, without anybody perceiving quite when, a little coal store began to thrive just opposite the brothels in Vig Street; a store which quickly raised sufficient capital for a new shop, just ten yards further up, selling goose feathers, inscribed with the name of Selma Grün. Soon afterwards, the brothers and sisters began to arrive, and each member of the family was given enough capital to set up in some small business. "We must live in obscurity," Selma advised every one of them, "we must ignore everything and everyone. What use is it to study, or to think?" I can remember that, through her metal teeth, Selma was still lisping to her grandchildren the same sweeping denials of conscience, even in quite recent years.

Another of her commandments was the respectful greeting to be bestowed on everyone, even avowed enemies. "Greet the gentleman!" she would murmur under her breath to her brothers and sisters, when walking in the street with them, and her advice was accompanied by terrible pinches on the arms or sides of whoever fell short in this regard. These greetings were perhaps the only form of human communication known to Selma. She never willingly talked to anyone, unless on business or to give orders. She rarely did anything with her own hands. "Give me the pan," she would say to one of her brothers, even if the saucepan was within easy reach. "Shut the door!" she would command, even to her own father. She must have possessed some mysterious force, if everyone thus obeyed her without argument. But whenever she greeted someone, a sudden jovial expression would suffuse her face and sometimes remain there for several minutes, past the point of being called for. In the early days, before she got so fat, she used to walk in the street with pleasure. Every evening she would follow People's Theatre Street, and only that one, just for the sake of being able to greet the passers-by. In this way, she soon established a reputation for being a magnanimous and courteous person. Because it must be said that she didn't disdain to offer smiles and other signs of cordiality even to the most hardened drunkards in the quarter.

"You never know. One day we may need even them." As for the owners of the shops and the brothels! With them she was all smarmy, and her well-instructed brothers looked like so many reeds, so energetically did they bow. By means of these exchanges of courtesy, her acquaintance soon spread to the whole of the Eighth District. Through this acquaintance, and with the aid of a broker, her brothers and sisters were all married off in the space of a few years. She, the eldest, got married last of all. As a husband for her, her father produced one of his own rivals, a canvas-sack merchant called Armin Heimann, a good Jew with a reputation for diligence and silence. Selma hated him from the very first day of the marriage, as she would perhaps have hated any other man. Recently, his relatives have told me that Selma wouldn't even greet him. Coming back from work, she would eat something and then withdraw to the furthest corner of her remote and obscure realm. They had a daughter, Rachel for the community and Regina for the Registry Office. And her too Selma set about instructing, with mingled patience and ferocity, in all her commandments. "Greet the gentleman!" she would hiss, turning towards the girl with blazing eyes. When the child reached four years of age, Selma thought fit to demonstrate her own regal superiority and her own feelings towards the family. One evening, screaming at the top of her incredibly piercing voice, she broke a pot full of excrement and urine over her husband's head, and then, over Rachel's, a can full of goose-fat. Poor Armin escaped from Selma's domination by contracting Spanish Fever, which carried him off in a few days.

"Always have a little money in your pocket. It may be useful if you need to go to the lavatory." This instruction of Selma's probably dated from the end of the Great War. Evidently a certain degree of poverty must have descended on the family, if members of it were going around with empty pockets. However, be that as it may, this is the very epoch from which we must date Selma's extreme obesity. By the time I knew her, she was no longer capable of waddling a hundred yards. She proceeded with a grand slowness, wobbling enormous haunches which were hidden under black skirts and overalls. Rather than walk, she seemed to crawl. Food, like the world itself, did not please or satisfy her; she ate little, but that little she held in her intestines for days. If, during the thirty yards that stretched from the shop to the house, she happened to feel the need of relieving herself, it would be a crisis for her. She would give exaggerated tips to the janitors, just to cancel the shame of having to use their lavatories.

Every evening she cooked huge quantities of food, which she then distributed among her relatives and the Gypsies who lived in their block. On Sundays there were pastries in abundance, six or seven different varieties, made with poppyseed, walnuts, grated cabbage, apples or cherries. Selma's brothers and sisters had her same attitudes regarding food. Her eldest brother Michael, for example, died some forty years later from occlusion of the intestines, after a good five operations on his digestive tract. When, already old, they would take my hand to go walking, they would often pause to make an anguished search for a cafe or the doorway of a relative's house. Provided that there were no stairs to go up or down, for all the Grüns suffered from vertigo. Going to visit some of their relatives, they would traverse the stairwell with their faces turned to the wall, like the condemned, to avoid the terrible attraction of emptiness and its accompanying invitation to throw up. Over the years, Selma had striven to reduce to the minimum any space around her and any necessity of movement. She no longer went to the synagogue, to avoid having to climb to the women's gallery, poised up above the main hall. Against these sufferings Selma set her money, not as a symbol of power, but as a barrier to hold back the threat of real physical disability and the world that represented. Having a little change in one's pocket for the lavatory signified that one was confronting a far greater danger: that of living. "You'll be sorry, if you don't pay attention to me," she exclaimed one day, seeing me smiling at her homilies. "*Ho lile wehas! God forbid!* You might get some terrible stomach trouble!" It was clear from her comments that she regarded this organ as representing the universe, with all its imperfections. In Selma's admonitions there was a veiled criticism of the handiwork of God.

Only in music did she find some relief and a few moments of delight. Music for her was represented by the Gypsy players who lived all around her. Her dominion extended to them also. With gifts of food and tips she had won their sympathy, and with her terrific cries had gained also their fear and reverence. "Excellent Madam," she was hailed by the old singers, made hoarse by the smoke of nightclubs and restaurants; or else, "Noble Madam." Up from the courtyard to Selma's little flat floated the continual, swirling music of violins and cimbalons. Occasionally, Selma would grow exasperated by the music and would send her daughter to shut them up. But on events like the Jewish festivals, or weddings or births, she would arrange for not just a band but a whole orchestra of Gypsy musicians. Her payments were lavish. Selma believed that the range of musical expression was universal. For her, it represented pleasure of the highest order. "You must study music," she had continued to urge generation after generation of youngsters who, during the several decades of her "reign", had passed before her eyes. "With music you'll be sure of your bread, even amongst the Hottentots." With verbal communication she wasn't that much at home, truth to tell: only a few oaths, perfectly pronounced in seven or eight languages. For the rest, she could chew out only a little Slovak, twenty or so expressions in Yiddish, and as for Hungarian, she was continually mixing it up with Romanian. Music didn't demand any such effort from her; the glissandos, tempos, trills and double chordings of Gypsy music expressed everything for her, without ever passing into the forbidden territory of thought. With the art of playing, even an illiterate could conquer the world. In those days, which were neither very soft nor very harsh, to conquer the world meant to survive without too much hardship. A just interpretation of Selma's famous precepts about music had preserved various youths of the Eighth District from painful disillusionments, and even from suicide. Selma believed in a music which was material and terrestrial. Celestial music was for her inimitable and unattainable; composing that would have been blasphemous. The creation of "divine" music has never been the aim of Jewish composers; among them there have never been, fortunately, any figures of titanic grandeur. But there are swarms of excellent instrumentalists. Selma's precept "You must study music" was the only true piety in her decalogue; in all the rest there were the seeds of corruption and of a fearful dark realism.

Which were manifested in her when she got acquainted with and married a decayed nobleman from Bukovina, giving up - in accordance with laws of that time - the faith of her fathers. This occurred at the end of the great slump.

Selma, with her sisters and brothers, had by now taken possession of a whole row of stalls in the Teleky Square Market. But instead of collaborating among themselves in the sale of plucked geese, these blood-relations, hitherto so closely united, became the most ferocious competitors. "Never trust anyone, not even your own brother," Selma would tirelessly repeat to herself, to the customers she managed to secure, and to the neighbouring stallholder, Mr Jakabffy. He who had once owned restaurants in Cluj was now pushed by fate to the capital, to become a goose-dealer alongside his wife, who was almost as fat as Selma. Mr Jakabffy, apart from being of noble stock, as attested by the final *y* in his name, was also quite a cultivated man. He knew by heart whole chunks of epic and patriotic poems of the nineteenth century, and used to play chess rather well. His failure as a restauranteur was perhaps due to his very cultivation. Within a year or two of his acquaintance with Selma, the poor man's wife fell ill with leukaemia. Selma set about nursing the dying woman with the dedication of a saint, devoting every free moment to her, helping her to wash, mopping the sweat from her face with her own hands - and that face was, it seems, still beautiful, like that of a china doll. Every day, she carried to her the most tasty food from her own kitchen. Then the fat neighbour died, and within the space of a few months, all according to plan, Selma married the widower, becoming at one blow a noblewoman and a Christian, leaving behind her the petty Jewish trader she had been.

From the religious point of view, the conversion ceremony seemed to Selma a real farce, as she told me years later; but from, let us say, the political angle, she seemed to be the focus of a solemn coronation, not to mention the annexation of a new, large and fertile kingdom. One hundred and twenty Gypsies played for the three days and three nights of Selma's wedding, and the houses of all the Jews and Gypsies of Matyas Square, where the couple were to live in a one-room apartment with kitchen, were flooded with good food and fine sweets. Her daughter Rachel also took part in the festivities; she had meanwhile married a footballer from Bratislava. Her brothers and sisters participated likewise, with their spouses and their children, along with her father, although he was very ill at the time. Suddenly and inexplicably peace returned amongst all of them. Selma's betrayal was not taken too seriously or bitterly by the family. It was considered, rather, as a benevolent act, one of generous solidarity and masterly astuteness, and as it was in line with all the laws hitherto promulgated by Selma herself, it could only reinforce her position of dominance. Quarrels over the customers ceased, or at least were confined to mild remonstrances, and even if Selma could no longer appear at the synagogue, she certainly did not forget to cook her sweets for the Jewish festivals, or even to fast at Kippur. As for the nobleman, he could do exactly as he pleased; his role had already been played. As a husband he was not permitted to touch even with a finger, supposing he should want to, his own wife. And, as they had always done, they continued to address one another quite formally. But over all this apparent peace spread the poison of the coming universal disenchantment.

The precept of not trusting even your own brothers had taken root in the hearts of the whole family, and more than one marriage, more than one friendship, had subsequently to pay for it. Several decades later, before my brothers and I left our native land for ever, old Selma weepingly underlined, among all her precepts, this one: "Never trust anyone." I confronted the world, like all disciples born under Selma's rule, with the awareness that I was walking in the midst of my assassins. The sixth commandment was born at the time of the most terrible trials: "Do for others what you feel inclined to do, and for yourself do always the impossible." Despite the apparently sordid egotism of this saying, it does not lack a certain grandeur and sanctity, whilst coming events were to prove its soundness,.

The racial laws came into force. Selma's brothers and sisters, her in-laws and their children, all sewed the yellow star upon their breasts, not yet knowing that this was the signal for the Angel of Death. Selma herself was exempt from this obligation. From the height of her acquired Aryan status, she would order her faithful servant, her husband, now to buy forged safe-conducts for her brothers and brothers-in-law, now to buy clothing for them, now to carry secret messages in the dark hours to relatives already pressed into labour and bound for Russia to dig trenches. In those tragic days, Selma did for others what she felt inclined to do - a great deal, to tell the truth. And even the husband, cross-examined by the prostitutes of their block, all of them married now to some barber or cobbler, as to why he exposed himself so light-heartedly to all these dangers, would answer with Selma's motto. He practically never used words of his own. When he was not engaged in carrying out one of his wife's commands, he would pace around their one room, repeating to himself some nonsense syllables like *hokus-pokus* or *etele-petele,* just to pass the time. Which was passing anyway, turning inexorably towards the worst. The safe-conducts, which had cost

Selma a fortune, didn't win any recognition from the authorities. The men went off in the labour gangs, carrying in their knapsacks a little spare linen and a few jars of marmalade; they were confident of returning quite soon, whilst their wives and children, weeping over this temporary separation, were no less sanguine.

Then Selma's sisters and her daughter Rachel, now the mother of three children, were shut into the artificial ghetto built by the German troops who had entered the city. Now came the time for Selma to practise the second part of her precept: "...for yourself do always the impossible," demonstrating the grandeur of her reign, no longer in acts of piety, but in gestures of absolute value.

During the last months of the war, Selma unexpectedly fell sick. Her illness was very serious; acute nephritis, if I remember rightly. Doctors and medicines were not to be found, and her husband paced the city amid the patter of bullets, with corpses piled at every corner and a pitiless snow which fell as if it wanted to bury the world. In the end, he had to give up. Selma believed herself near death. With her huge bulk, she lay in bed like a great beast in captivity. The husband watched her in silence, while a neighbour, the ex-prostitute who called her "Mamma" in recognition of some small loans and even an inheritance, changed her *prisniz,* that is, the cold compresses upon her breast, designed to draw out the fever. Those two hundred and eighty pounds of malodorous flesh were trembling beneath the lashes of sickness and delirium.

One freezing morning in December, Selma unexpectedly sat up in bed and ordered her husband in a calm voice to go and look for a rabbi who could rid her of the curse of conversion, and then to gather together in the house all her sisters, her daughter and her grandchildren. She wanted her solemn return to the bosom of the people of Israel to take place under their eyes. Little did it matter that leaving the ghetto could mean summary execution for them; they would find the safest means to obey her call. Then means must be found - who knew how, seeing that the community was already three-parts exterminated - to purchase a tomb in the Jewish cemetery and to find a purifier of the dead. Selma wanted to die as a good Jewess, so as to found her kingdom anew in the hereafter. The impossible, that's exactly what Selma was asking for.

The order was peremptory, and it was the duty of her husband to carry it out point by point. Years later, whenever he told this story, the poor man's visage would assume the terror-painted features of that day, and he would openly confess his helplessness before the majesty of his wife; but it was just that boundless admiration for her that helped him to a decision. Selma, seeing him hesitate, let out several horrifying yells which resounded through the courtyard like the cries of vampires. Shaking like the monstrous Behemoth on the Day of Judgement, she started chucking furniture, plates, whatever fell under her hand. In the face of Selma's rage, the husband no longer dreamt of obstacles; he was more scared of her than of death itself. Braving many times the dangers of arrest and execution, he carried out all that had been demanded of him, except the purchase of the tomb and the summoning of the purifier of corpses. He furnished the rabbi and Selma's relatives with green hoods and one day, after darkness had fallen, he got them out of the ghetto. As soon as the ceremony was over, they disappeared just as they had come, into a darkness which for many of them might prove eternal. Selma then lay back on the pillows and closed her eyes.

She opened them again when the war was over, and all her family was once more united around her bed to pray for her recovery. Her brothers, her sisters, her daughter and her grandchildren had all miraculously survived; only two brothers-in-law failed to answer the call, both of them lost in the Russian camps. Selma never ceased to believe that the salvation of her dear ones was due to her double conversion, and she held fast for the rest of her life to her precept of doing the impossible for oneself, for the benefit of others.

The sayings "Know a language and you know a man" and "Believe in the police as in yourself" were, one way or another, key items in the credo of Selma Grün. The first, in apparent contradiction to all her pronouncements about music and to her obvious verbal deficiencies, was nevertheless an integral and logical part of her philosophy. If Selma spoke virtually no language, this was because she despised them all. She knew the workings of the world, and she knew them to be both fragile and downright absurd. To describe them, it was enough to have a dozen words and a few gestures. In that sense, Selma would have been capable of speaking all the seventy languages of the world spoken of in the Talmud, but for her it just wasn't worthwhile. Once she was cured, she offered herself as an interpreter to the Soviet troops, and with her atrocious Slovak she made herself well understood by the Russian and Mongol soldiers. One day, Matyas Square watched in astonishment as a whole platoon went into Selma's house loaded with jams, tinned meat, sugar, lard and flour. "All that, in exchange for a little gold-plated watch!" Selma declared with pride. She distributed all this God-given produce among her family and neighbours, keeping only the barest necessities for her husband and herself. When I asked her in stupefaction and alarm how she had done it, she replied, "Know a language and you know a man," stuffing a piece of bread into my mouth.

Within a year, she took up English lessons from an old *goyte* greengrocer who had returned from Detroit after ten fruitless years of emigration. *"Vaduju vant tu iit?"* Selma had scribbled in a notebook which she always kept in a pocket of her apron, and in a margin of the same she had written in pencil: *"Hau mach muni?"* With these few words, she had decided to confront the New World and subjugate it also. Her love of ignorance had made her capable of measuring herself against the unknown at any moment. For this trait she was much hated, but also much admired by her subjects, infinitely more inept than herself. Following Selma's teachings, her grandchildren, scattered throughout the world, have become real polyglots, but because they long to penetrate the deepest secrets of languages and peoples, they now live enclosed in their own sterile solitude of interpretation. Had they listened to another of Selma's admonitions: "At the end of all there is only one language, that of God," perhaps they would be the happier for it. Or perhaps more desperate still.

As for her blind faith in the forces of law and order, this was based on the most ancient principles. Selma respected all forms of constituted authority, in order to be respected herself. But there was more to it than that. If her respectful greetings were adequately reciprocated by the police of the Eighth District, her gifts of goose-breast, or sometimes of a whole bird, obliged these simple sons of the peasantry to show a certain warmth. But Selma had never attempted to corrupt them; she only sought protection from wrongdoers and competitors. The strange inner force that issued from her personality constrained these guardians of order to show her a certain respect and even to overlook the fact that she, whether converted or not, was still a Jewess. Her unlimited faith in the police also extended the reign of Selma.

One day, a plainclothes agent knocked at her door, flashed a card, and demanded that she show the hiding place of her gold objects and her dollars; the new Communist regime did not permit the holding of such riches. Selma offered no resistance, no protest. She pulled a package from a cupboard drawer and offered it to him. She let herself be robbed. Only when the robber had gone did she notice that the card he had produced was a simple tram permit. She called the police. After a trial lasting a few minutes, he was condemned to pay a modest fine; after all, the objects of the offence, the gold and dollars, had disappeared. His confession of guilt also mitigated the offence.

Then even the new order began to have its upheavals, and all the younger generation abandoned the Eighth District, and the country. Selma's kingdom was left deserted.

It made no sense to continue her dominion over three or four old and sick subjects. There was still one more task to be performed. Selma called a retired police captain, her former client and judge. She promised him her own inheritance - house, furniture, money - if he succeeded in bringing her grandchildren, her very life's blood, back to Hungary. The old man didn't say no; he took a small advance and vanished forever from the Eighth District. Selma now threw open her innards to the onset of sickness. She developed a tumour in her throat and another in the rectum, close to the anus; at the two gateways of that huge organism.

"The best medicine is death," had always been her motto. She could never tolerate the idea of anyone messing about with that perfect unity which her deformed body represented. No doctors or charlatans were permitted in her realm. Unlike her brother, who had endured being cut to pieces before his death, Selma refused even to be admitted to a hospital. She died in the darkness of her own house. She entrusted the tenth commandment to her last breath: "Close the door, so that life doesn't run away!"

IN HIS OWN IMAGE
AND LIKENESS

After twenty years of silence and strange mumbling, he suddenly began to speak in a clear, firm voice. Doctor Iwan has taken down his words, recording them with reasonable fidelity in his notebooks.

He spoke for about half an hour before lapsing again into silence, this time for ever.

"My name is Robert Leuchtner. I was 'touched' from birth, according to my cousins, but I'm not really convinced of it. It's true my mother told me I was born with my head open at the back, and that I was operated on right away, but now I'm forty-two and I can reason perfectly well. Dr Geldrich comes to see me sometimes, makes me walk up and down, taps my knee with a hammer and asks me to do mathematical calculations. I can do these alright, even if I'm a bit slow. I have a star-like gait, the doctor says, and continually rotate my head around a point in the cervix. Every now and again, I faint for a few minutes, but up to now, *gläubt zi Gott*, nothing bad has happened to me in falling. It's true that I could hit my head on some sharp corner or tumble over the railings into the void. However, these attacks of mine, which Dr Geldrich calls 'pseudo-epileptic fits', arrive practically without warning. All at once, I begin to see a big black circle, and I feel an emptiness which mounts from my stomach into my chest, then right up to my head. When I come to, I may find myself under the table, or under a chair, or with my head against the lavatory door.

I'm very fond of girls. In our building, in Little Transport Street, there are two or three of them: one's a blonde and lives downstairs; the other's a brunette, with long plaited hair, and I always see her coming downstairs in the morning when she's going to school.

She must live on the third or fourth floor. I look at her from below, to catch a glimpse of her long legs and panties. Only the blonde is Jewish; the other one is a *schikse.*

I have studied at school, and I can read and write very well, but I don't enjoy doing it. Even in the school for backward children, where I went for ten years, I preferred gazing out the window to looking at a sheet of white paper, full of little black ants which formed a word or a sentence when put in rows. When I reached the third or fourth sentence of a lesson or a composition, I usually couldn't remember what I had written earlier. Now this happens to me even more often, so I don't read or write any more. I've never managed to learn the Hebrew characters. The prayers were taught to me by Rabbi Stern. I know only one: *Baruh atto adonaj.*

I like eating very much, but I hate the filthiness of knives and forks. Mother's a very good cook. Most of all, I like goose-meat broth with tagliatelle, and gnocchi made with semolina or with mazos, the last being especially for our Seder feast, our Passover supper. I spend Seder with a niece of my mother's, who has three children and a husband. The husband isn't an *oischer* but is always very elegant and reads the prayers beautifully in Hebrew. My three cousins are three very likeable boys, but their hands are always filthy because they play lots of football and don't wash them afterwards. And so they're always touching that ball, which is covered with mud and market refuse, because they go to play between the stalls after closing time. That's why I always carry my own cutlery in the inside pocket of my jacket. I clean it myself, every morning.

Recently I have begun fainting more often. My mother is practically never at home when I faint. A brother-in-law of hers, who lives with us, keeps an eye on me; Uncle Abraham, an old typographer, very fat and bald, who never goes to the temple. But he goes a lot to the circus and the hippodrome. He can imitate with his mouth the sounds of the balalaika, the trumpet and the ocarina. He's retired and he shits through his side, because years ago he had cancer of the intestines. It's he who picks me up when I fall at home and holds my hands still, because during these fainting fits my muscles tremble uncontrollably. Sometimes I go to the hippodrome with him. If he wins a bit of money he's very kind to me. He buys me sweets or chocolates, or two or three pickled gherkins. If he loses he doesn't dare go home straight away, and I have to walk with him for hours and hours. On these occasions, he usually goes to the cemetery on Kerepes Road to pick up carob beans and heaps of chestnuts, then husks them and throws them away. I do the same.

I'd like to have a child. Yes! I even know how it's done.

My cousins explained it to me, even though they're younger than me. My father, who died during the war, never told me about it. My mother never talks about these things either, and when I ask her to explain them, she always starts laughing. So I don't insist. Often in the evenings, when my mother comes home tired from work and soon goes to bed, I see her undressing and I like seeing her white skin and her big breasts. I'd love to touch them some time, but up to now I haven't had the courage. I have thought I could perhaps have a baby with Rachel. Whenever she looks down into the courtyard, or walks around the gallery inside, I run to get my accordion and begin to play it as loud as I can. I studied music with an old teacher my mother knew in the market. She gave him a dresser and a couple of geese, because he gave me lessons for at least six months. When she gave him a third goose, whose liver had been fattened, this teacher not only took me on as his pupil but declared that I was very musical.

He taught me to read the notes and to play them on the accordion. Mother bought me a beautiful red and black accordion, made by Hohner. She loves me very much, my mother does, and is always saying that she lives only for me; that if it wasn't for me, nothing else in life would matter to her.

How odd. Yet I know that I'm not very good to look at. In these last few years my back has become bent, and if I don't shave twice a day I always sprout ugly black, thick hairs on my cheeks. Mother always says that I'm a divine blessing for her, just because I'm like this. I could try to have a baby with my aunt, who also lives with us, but I don't like her much because she's so short and dresses so

72

badly, even though she's a dressmaker. She often works at home, on an old Singer machine. Sometimes she goes out for the whole afternoon, because she has to go and fit dresses at the house of some woman who wouldn't trouble herself to come here for anything in the world. My aunt is very good to me. She washes my pants when I foul them and clips the hairs that sprout from my ears. What's more, I'm extremely hairy, and when I look at myself in the mirror, naked, I look to myself more like a dog or a sheep, or even a monkey. Only that these animals don't wear a cap, whereas I always do, even when I'm sleeping. I was taught this by Rabbi Stern, who also taught me that God is always watching us, so we should keep our heads always covered. Another rabbi, who came after him, said to me that it's useless hatching lice in this way and that the Spriptures don't say anywhere that we must always cover our heads. But I have a nice beret of Irish wool, with a little peak, that suits me very well. Apart from which, it covers my neck, where everyone could otherwise see the scars that I've carried since the second day of my life.

Some time ago a certain man came to visit our house. You could see from a mile off that he was a *goy*. He wanted to know my profession. There was a long silence, then my mother asked, "But don't you see how he is?" Still, the man insisted on asking my profession and even got angry, because the state didn't permit anyone to be unemployed. The unemployed were all delinquents, parasites or secret exploiters. Then mother began to yell. I had never heard her shout like that. She went all red and her hands began shaking. My aunt, on the contrary, spoke very calmly, and at a certain point she suddenly began to

73

whisper. She put a hundred-florin note into the man's hand, which he held for a minute and then left on the table. At this point my uncle returned from the race track; he explained everything to the man, even using some Latin words. Uncle is very well-informed; as a typographer he's had through his hands manuscripts by the greatest poets and authors, and he could always understand everything, besides correcting the errors of grammar or spelling. That man never came back again. I don't want to go to work, not for all the gold in the world. I'm happy looking at the sun on the galleries and the girls going up and down stairs. I also like hearing the noise of the tram through the closed windows and the voices of the hawkers in the courtyard, when they come selling pumice-stone, or to repair the big wash basin or any broken windows.

I especially like to hear the husky voices of the ice-vendors. There's something else I like, but which I can't confess to anyone. Before getting up in the morning to get dressed, I often stay under the covers and stroke myself between the legs. Then my penis gets hard and after a while some white liquid comes out of it. My cousins tell me that in this liquid there are heaps of children who are only waiting to be put between the legs of a girl or a woman, so they can climb up to her belly and come out into the world, after five or six months of growth. I would already have produced countless children, if all that always happened. I feel bad to think of all those children dying between the sheets and the blanket. Perhaps they'll lie between the goose-feathers sewn into the coverlet, and wait to come out into the world. They could be more numerous than all the men living on earth, and then half of them

74

would be my children. I've only spoken of all this once, up to now, one Friday evening with Rabbi Stern. He looked at me silently for a while, then said nobody on earth has so many children. Only God possesses so many souls, all made in His image and likeness. What did he mean to tell me by saying that?

The other day Uncle took me to the ground floor of a house two blocks away from ours, on the corner of Teleky Square. It had once been one of our temples. Now it has become a hall for cultural gatherings. A comrade spoke about the economic situation and the purges which must be made in the Party. There were too many members and some of them were people unworthy of belonging, by reason of their origin or background. After this, my cousin recited "Verses of a Son of the Proletariat" by Endre Ady and was loudly applauded. He had put on a moth-eaten sweater and a pair of broken shoes. Instead of laces, he had put in a couple of old straws. Then somebody announced that I would play some popular tunes on the accordion and Uncle took me up the little platform from which the comrade had spoken. I played "La Paloma" and "My little boat is rocking on the Danube", and I got lots of applause. Every time they applauded I began playing again, but always one of these two pieces, which were the only ones I knew by heart. I played for maybe half an hour, until Uncle came to pull me off the platform and I heard everyone laugh, partly from pleasure and a little from having been taken in. They gave me fifteen florins for my show and urged me to learn some other pieces, so that I could play at the next cultural meeting and earn some more money. After me, a man went up to the platform to read loudly some phrases which must be chanted next May Day, and everybody repeated them in chorus.

Yesterday something very strange happened to me that I never experienced before and that terrified me. I was just waking up in my bed, which is made up for me with such love by my mother and aunt, who have to change the sheets almost every day because I so often piss in them during the night. The door opened very slowly and I saw a horribly ugly person enter the room, with its hair standing on end and a knife in its hand. I began yelling at the top of my voice, so loudly that my throat still hurts, but this person still kept on approaching, so I got out of bed, throwing myself upon this creature more horrible than any devil, seizing its hand and biting it, so that it couldn't do me any harm. I heard a loud cry and was thrust backwards so violently that I fell on the bed. When I reopened my eyes, my mother was standing by the bed. There was a yellow liquid spilt on the floor, together with bits of a broken cup. My mother was weeping and kept asking me insistently:

"But what happened to you, my love?"

"Nothing," I replied.

"How do you mean, nothing? You bit me on the hand here, look! What have I done to deserve this?"

Her hand was all bloody and I couldn't explain to myself why I hadn't recognized her. I was really frightened by all this; rather than have a dibbuk or some animal come to live inside me without my knowledge, I'd prefer to die.

So far I've seen only one person die, a brother of my mother's who was a waiter in a restaurant and had suffered from asthma since he was a child. He lived here with us for several years, always coming home very late at night, even after eleven, and always smelling of wine and grease. In the mornings he used to get up after me and walk around the house in his slippers, breathing with difficulty and coughing horribly. Whenever I fainted, he would just leave me on the floor, because he hadn't the strength to pull me up. He did try once, but he too ended up on the floor, breaking his head open on the edge of the kitchen stove. I, on the other hand, have never broken anything because, according to Rabbi Stern, God holds His hand over my head.

I don't know if that was the cause, but soon things went as I had long feared they would. When this uncle died, he had been in bed for about a year, and the other uncle had been giving him two injections every day of some medicine called morphine. After these injections he would feel a little better; he would get up, eat something, go to the lavatory, but then begin again with his heavy breathing and suffocating cough. His breathing was so noisy that sometimes I couldn't sleep at night. During the last week, Uncle Abraham no longer left the bedside of his sick brother-in-law. He just gave him injections and waited. One night, I was sitting up with him and I suddenly heard in the darkness, from the end of the bed, a groaning cry: "I'm dying, I'm dying!"

Perhaps because Uncle Abraham was a bit deaf, having worked in a printing house all his life, he heard something quite different and said to him, "It doesn't matter, it doesn't matter." "But why doesn't it matter?" asked a small voice from the end of the bed, and then followed a long silence until dawn. When it grew light, Uncle Abraham woke up and gave another injection, but the medicine poured out again from the leg, because the patient was already dead.

Now that I sometimes don't recognize my mother any more, nor Aunt nor Uncle, I'm afraid that I may be equally misunderstood some day, because of my condition and because of the dibbuk or the animal which has hidden inside me.

I don't want to believe that my mother wants to be rid of me, as I overheard the other day. They were all in the kitchen and I wanted to join them, when I realized they were talking about me. I cocked my ears and I heard Uncle Abraham's voice saying that he was now quite weak from looking after me and that Mother could no longer depend on him to take care of me as in the past, because he was getting really ill. Then he named an institution.

If Mother does such a thing, I shall die right away; and then I'll return inside her to haunt her for the rest of her days, like the fiercest of dibbuks.

I can do lots of good things, like reading and writing and playing the accordion, and I love my mother so much, and my aunt and my cousins. So why should I have to become a dikkuk? I also love Rachel and perhaps one day I'll be able to marry her and have children.

Among my mother's nephews, no one in the family has any children; they are all sickly and are always quarrelling among themselves. Perhaps they don't have any of that white liquid, whose scientific name I don't remember, although my cousins did tell it to me.

I have enough of it to fill the whole Eighth District, to

78

fill the whole city and the whole world with children, in my own image and likeness. Rabbi Stern can't stop me doing it. Perhaps he too thinks I should be sent to that institution, just because I couldn't perform my *bar-mizvà*.

Just now I'm learning by heart the music of the song "My Yiddish Mother" and I want to play it at the next cultural meeting. Then I shall earn another fifteen florins and will also prove my usefulness to the state. But first I'll play to Mother; then she'll understand what I want to tell her. They're always telling me that they can't understand a thing when I talk, that they hear nothing but an ugly mumbling. But I speak every word clearly and I suspect that for one reason or another, such as the printing house, or the tram, or the clamour of the market, the whole family has become deaf. To their ears, it must be just like the black circle that I'm beginning to see on the walls, above the tabernacle, in the temple, whenever misfortune is coming, and even in the sky when I raise my head. I'm terrified that one day, when I see that black circle growing ever larger, till it covers the whole of the Eighth District, *Gott behüte,* God forbid, I shan't wake up again after my fainting fit."

He died two days after admission, from natural causes. His mother dreamt of him every night for three years, until she too expired.

RACHEL'S MEMORY

It's an arid, inhospitable country in which Rachel lives. Few people are seen there. Those who pass by make a few remarks and then disappear. She sleeps late and when she awakes the sunset is all around her. If she glimpses someone in the cold, brief twilight, she tries to prepare herself for the occasion, behave as the case might require, nod or offer some short comment, quote a proverb. Otherwise, she just gazes into emptiness, pronounces some reflections on life in a dreamy voice, heaps insults on a ghost from the past, falls asleep again, bewails her lot.

I shan't talk about her permanent address, not knowing how to describe it. It's in a continental country, with its own climate and its own problems. But I'll speak of her world, of what some would call her inner landscape, even though it's sometimes too delicate a matter to distinguish between the inner and the outer.

It is there, in her spirit so to speak, that the sunlight seems spent, leaving behind only a few flakes of light. I spoke some time ago of the big red lips of one of my friends who paid her a visit, and the miracle of meeting him again, just by chance, in a cafe. But these are belated will-o'-the-wisps, offering no hope.

I too was once part of that world. I shared it, and at the

same time I was that world, object and subject together. And yet it wasn't granted me to know what it was like. I had nothing to compare it with. Now I have only a confused recollection of it; more of how arid it was and, yes, rather dark. But in the meantime, even in my personal world, it's grown dark, and perhaps it's this latter obscurity that stretches behind me, towards the past.

It's difficult to make an inventory of the things that lay in Rachel's memory, in her world.

In an old photo which shows her as an adolescent, her eyes are already suffering and timid, a long face without any particular charm, stiff arms and legs. The girl was harshly treated by a severe and punitive mother who, as Rachel has recently told me again, made her kneel on kernels of corn to increase her torments. What appalling heredity, what ancestor or what circumstances pushed this woman to mould her daughter in that way, I shall never know. But the plant produced bad fruit, as far as the second and perhaps the third generation.

In the chamber of her wrongs this was, however, only the first step.

Rachel always remembers her first job: typing for some lawyer, who kept feeling her up. Then followed short spells with traders, who paid her little; they were lacking in proper respect and didn't sufficiently appreciate her. And her adolescence finished there; because, these attempts at independent work having failed, she found herself back with her mother, as a goose-girl in the business which that lady had meanwhile opened. These must have been trying days for Rachel. I knew her mother and was frightened of her, of her cruel ways and the fierce pinches she gave to the arms of any child who annoyed her.

After her mother's death, Rachel visited the cemetery for twenty-five years, unfailingly, at least once a week, to pay homage at her tomb, leaving a pebble there and breathing words of respect and regret.

Then came her marriage, the circumstances of which offered an interminable family comedy. Isaac, the husband, always claimed that he had married Rachel against his will, almost at his parents' direction. Rachel claimed the opposite; that all the resistance had been on her mother's part and her own. In any event, it must have been like a liberation for her. From the time when my memory begins to emerge distinctly, I recall her as being a happy young woman. Happy to have found a husband ("She was an intelligent girl, but nobody would have asked her to dance," an aunt once said of her) and to have brought children into the world. During the week she worked hard, still with the geese. On Fridays she prepared the supper for the festival: fish soup, a little wine, lighted candles on the table, the saying of prayers. Sometimes she sang.

The war made her regret everything. It carried off her husband and her children; it also separated her from her mother. She was in the process of being deported: "As we filed along the street, a tram conductor snatched away my coat. He said I wouldn't need it any longer, the devil, that I could just go and rot." So she told it. It was then that she tried, for the first time, to close the emporium of memory. She took twenty tranquillizers, and had to be cleared out with a stomach pump. "I only wanted to sleep. Someone told me that I'd be saved in that way, that they wouldn't carry me off." So she told it. And in fact, they didn't deport

83

her.

Once the war was over, however, this wiping of the slate was not without consequences. It was like a lesson to Rachel. After it, when the war was already well behind us, she strove to forget, not everything, as she had with pills, but the most necessary things. This was without the aid of pills. Whatever was not of use to her, or was at odds with her way of thinking, she excluded from her memory, and even from the world of perceptible objects. Innumerable times she seems to have lost the keys of her house, her sewing needles, her purse with all her money, even the big bunch of keys for the padlocks of her stall. Every time, minutes had to be spent hunting for them. Often, these items were found in the most unlikely places: in the house of some relative; in the kitchen under a meat plate; in her handbag, which she had already searched a hundred times. Her husband used to taunt her about it. To her irrational attitude, he would oppose an apparently extreme lucidity. "Before anything, let's reconstruct events," he began, "tell me where you have been during the last three hours." Then he would check all the places she had listed. If that didn't work, he would proceed to a minute, systematic search of the house. If he had understood more clearly the meaning of this forgetfulness, perhaps he would have managed to find swifter and more effective ways of helping both her and himself.

In this world of apparitions and vanishings, money played a particular role. Rachel was fond of money, and still fonder of profit. Banknotes didn't attract her particularly for the riches they represented. But every one of them was evidence of a little victory of hers: her success in extracting it from the hands of some customer, even if it was in exchange for merchandise. She would give her own soul to sell something. One of her children once reproached her savagely: "You offer your nicest smile to any customer who comes along," he said, "but you have nothing left for us." This reproof left an impression on her. But she didn't change. Persuading a passerby to spend: this was her great satisfaction in life, the fruit of her exercise of will. So every banknote became an ensign snatched from the enemy, a victory banner. But mixed with this infliction of punishment, she also felt confused sentiments of guilt, obscure sensations of fear. Every evening, when she got back from work, Rachel counted her money. The takings were wrapped in a tea-cloth; they were taken out of her shopping bag and spread upon the table. She held the greasy banknotes between her fingers, one by one, fixing them intently with a wrinkled brow. She let them fall into a basket placed on a chair, only to gather them up again and replace them in the cloth. She devoted such attention to this that she seemed to recognize them every one. I bet that she could remember from whom each note came, in exchange what, whether it represented a fair price or included a little cheating, and thanks to wheedling or flattery it had been parted with by its former owner. The fact is, Rachel never failed to pay the boldest compliments to both male and female purchasers. She would address them as "Fair Sir", "Dearest Madam", and so forth. She really gave her soul. Perhaps her sense of guilt came from that. Hardly ever, however, did two counts of the takings come out the same. Usually the second count came to a few notes less, either because it would have pleased Rachel to have made more profit, or perhaps because she had thought of something displeasing in the meantime, which made her squeeze the notes harder and not notice when two were stuck together. Then straight away she must count again, until she arrived at the same sum at least three times running. Only then did the money return to its cloth, to be deposited beside her bed in the shopping bag.

The husband adopted the habit of watching her, when not even a crumb of their former love was left. In the brutal struggle of the succeeding years, he played a cunning game. He had noted Rachel's uncertainty and made it his business to encourage it. Every evening, he pushed her into having doubts. The number of banknotes came out ever more erratically, and the difference between one count and the next grew ever wider. "But wasn't it three thousand florins?" asked the bewildered Rachel. "You said before that it was three thousand five hundred," Isaac rebutted. Sometimes there was more, sometimes less. The final proof of three identical running counts would come only late in the evening, when Rachel's eyes were scarcely open. It was through these interventions in his wife's numerical calculations that Isaac succeeded in building up a nice little pile of money. Palming a few banknotes had become a very slight risk. Rachel would express surprise when he came home with something new, a suit or a hat. "Oh, I saved up a bit, I've been smoking less," he would explain, and the incident was closed. She would stammer a few words and then fall silent. Because this had always been her strategy: to cancel things out. She even cancelled out her husband's mistress, the woman he had visited several times a week for over twenty years.

One enigma was the disappearance of a large sum of money from a wardrobe in the house. Several thousand florins were involved. Rachel immediately accused her husband, more with her eyes than with her words. "Where have they gone?" she asked him, gazing fixedly into space.

Isaac replied that these were all ravings, that this money had never existed, and if it had it was she who had hidden it so thoroughly that it could no longer be found. Or else, that she had taken it down to the shop. For several evenings the two went up and down the house searching, or pretending to do so. Until Rachel sat down weeping and uttering imprecations against fate.

"My God, my God, what a wretch I am! I should have died during the war!" she wailed repeatedly. After a while, the search was suspended, and every time the subject came up she would shrug her shoulders and exclaim, "I don't know what really happened!"

When it was no longer enough to make her husband vanish, Rachel began to transform him. We were seated in a cafe, she stuffed with tranquillizers and a bit stunned. The husband was following the passersby with his eyes. He turned his head imperceptibly at the passage of a good-looking woman. I saw Rachel's face contract, before she leant over to me and whispered: "Don't tell anyone that you've got hot pants. If you do, they'll arrest you." I was shaken by this obscure speech. Only much later did I grasp its subtle significance. Rachel had placed me, a friend of the family, in the position of her husband. She would have liked to shout at him: "If your trousers are on fire, at least don't show it in public!" But the voice and the courage had stuck in her throat.

Later, she was taken to a psychiatrist. She hadn't adjusted to the double loss of her husband and her goose-dealer's stall, expropriated by the state and turned into a public enterprise. That stall was her damnation and her happiness. Like her marriage. When a public official came to seal up the place, she fell on her knees and implored him, swearing she'd done nothing wrong. She believed the expropriation was the result of some fault on her part; she could think of no other explanation for such a heavy punishment. She kissed the official's shoes and begged for grace. She found it, briefly, in tranquillizers.

After that, I didn't manage to keep track of her for several years, in her world of delirium, desperation and long sleeps in the hospital. I had run away. Now I have begun to see her again, and her memory seems to me to have become a more orderly, and I dare say, cleaner place.

After a short spell working in a state-run delicatessen, Rachel went into retirement and her delirium diminished. The medicines have cleared her system of much destructive and dangerous rubbish, broken glass and cumbersome boulders, perilously balanced. Now everything is trim and ship-shape; the streets, if nothing else, are quiet and empty. So she can go backwards in tranquillity, right back to her childhood, and forwards again, to her old age. But the more she moves to and fro, the more she finds the same thing. A small wrong suffered as a child and a theft at her expense as an adult; her mother's lack of love and her husband's; a family war and a world war. Every so often she inspects these familiar episodes, taking care that no one should be missing when the hour comes to give account, the hour in which she will be able to present the list of the wrongs she has suffered and to obtain satisfaction. In the meantime, she goes on visiting the cemetery to pay homage to her "adored mother" and to visit her husband's tomb and ask his forgiveness for having made him suffer. And it's useless to ask whether she is more sincere when she blackens the memory of them both, or when she shows her own feelings of love before their remains. In her country one can never know what is theatre and what is life.

Among real objects, her most intense relationship is still with the geese, the eternal merchandise of her life. When she carries one of them home, already plucked, she will put it on the kitchen table, look at it, and then caress it for several minutes. Only after this will she begin to cut it up, using a very sharp knife.

Otherwise, her days are monotonous. Few people are seen there. Those who pass by make a few remarks and then disappear. She sleeps late and when she awakes, the sunset is all around her.

SCIOLET

Some months ago, when I was speeding down the autostrada of the South, I saw a strangely shaped, small red car slow down and stop ahead of me. I too slowed down. When I got close, I recognized one of those cheap cars so popular in Eastern Europe, the tiny Trabant. A man and a woman got out and sat themselves disconsolately on the roadside. I stopped and walked over to them, spurred more by curiosity than a genuine wish to help. When I reached to within a few yards of them, I stopped as if petrified. The man was holding in his hand an object that brought back to me in a flash the record of people and places that I had long forgotten, or so I believed after these many years. The memory was linked to one of the most humiliating and painful episodes of my life, one which marked me so deeply as to destroy my self-esteem for ever. If I'm still willing to press on with my life today, it's because of the indifference of an age which welcomes equally the weak and the strong, the good and the bad; the just and the unjust; only to thrust them all into the whirlpool of their own irresistible nullity.

The object I had seen that day was a simple tin can for preserving food. In big orange letters it carried the legend *sciolet.* Exactly so; the name of the old staple food of

Central European Jewry, the best, the most satisfying; made especially for the poor, who could keep it in their kitchens for three or four days, or even longer, without fear of its going bad.

It was a concoction of dried beans, eggs, rice and goose-flesh (sometimes beef or lamb instead), and was cooked in the oven in a big saucepan, its lid fastened with fine string to which was fastened a label bearing the name of the family who owned it. This was because the *sciolet* needed a whole night's cooking and was therefore placed in the big communal oven. No private house could burn and keep watch over a fire for that length of time. After cooking, all the ingredients would have blended together. The bones had become soft as butter, the boiled eggs had mingled with the beans, while the meat was reduced to tender strips and fibres. There was a whole cosmogony in this food (as in all food, for that matter): the world appeared there, if you think about, as on the first day of Creation, or as after that of Destruction. Obviously, the canning industry of Hungary, from which country the tourists came, had decided to manufacture it, not certainly for it symbolic value, but counting upon a still sufficiently numerous clientele, the Jews of Budapest.

This *sciolet,* or *scialet,* as it is pronounced in Yiddish, instead of arousing in me the memory of tender maternal caresses, as happened with a famous Jewish writer in France and a certain kind of biscuit, summoned before my eyes, almost in flesh and blood, the person I had hated most in childhood, someone I could consider my assassin: Tibor Schreiber. To say that he was the most impenitent swindler in the Eighth District in the years following the

Second World War is to say very little; in my eyes he always remained, beyond being a swindler, a real butcher whose victim I still feel myself, rightly or wrongly, to be.

I don't know exactly from which part of Europe his family hailed. I believe they were of Polish origin. Tibor's father was a printer, a man noted for his honesty and wide culture. I would like to talk about him also, but the memory of his son goads and pricks me like a thorn. How gladly would I forget his perfect white teeth, his thin little moustache, the sideburns growing halfway down his cheeks, and a head almost bald before he was thirty. He was about that age when I first knew him.

He was my third cousin, or something of the kind. Before the outbreak of the war, he had served for three years as a regular officer in the artillery, so as a small child I never saw him in our family circle. I knew of his existence, and that his father would have liked to have him at his side in the printing business. Then, with the war, came the persecutions. From being a non-commissioned officer in the artillery, Tibor Schreiber was sent straight to one of the labour gangs and carted off to Russia to dig trenches. He soon reappeared in Budapest, however. He had escaped dramatically from a collection centre, from which many Jews were later despatched to the ovens of Dachau and Mauthausen. After three years of military service and four of persecution, suffering and escape, he reappeared in the Eighth District at the end of the war as a man of proven mettle, very different from the ever-smiling boy he had once been. "My boy," he said to me the first time he took me on his knee, "life is like Ràkòczy Avenue: to begin with it's all theatre, in the middle it's a hospital,

93

and at the end a cemetery." He no longer believed in anything, considering human existence as one interminable series of mechanical acts, repeated with stupid regularity. Neither life nor death made any sense to him. To be in the world was a cruel joke, to be repaid with the fiercest lack of conscience.

He left off the printing trade and became a dealer. He appeared in our house for Seder and other Jewish festivals, always very elegant, with that eternal pipe in his mouth and his few hairs smoothed with brilliantine. He came with the prettiest Jewish girls in the quarter, all of them young, fresh and a little timid. One night I overheard my father whisper to my mother that Tibor Schreiber had taken the maidenheads of at least forty girls in the district. Apart from women, his main interests were clothes, nightclubs, cars and motorbikes. Of cars he possessed two and of motorbikes only one, but that was a powerful BMW, which counted as four. Tibor had become a regular *oischer,* a big spender without conscience or anxiety. Where did he get all this money from? Well, his scepticism had been rewarded, rather than punished. I too began to consider him, God knows why, as a sort of hero in the art of living.

"My boy," he said to me, during one Kippur fast, seeing me eye a piece of cake, "money is like the poppyseeds of that cake. When the flowers are dead and well dried, the wind breaks them and scatters the seeds; so new plants are born. You like to see those flowers when they are still red, I know, but their beauty will not serve you for anything." He was attracted only by the arid materialism of money. He had banished from his heart any sentiment which didn't bring with it some economic advantage. He

94

had chosen his own parents as his first victims when he set out to sell gold-plated rings and bracelets, as if they were eighteen carat. Then his clientele slowly grew. Later on, Tibor began to buy real gold articles on the black market, only to sell them the same day at ten times the price. He began to trade in cloth as well, pushing as genuine Irish woollens certain materials left in the shops from before the war; materials which were really of Czech or Polish origin. He also began to hoard dollars, speculating on the fluctuations of the exchange rate. He spent his days in the cafes, striking deals, making offers and pocketing money. In the evenings, he roared through the streets of the Eighth District on his motorbike, looking for new girls to take out to dinner, to dances, and then to the apartment he had rented along with a friend, solely as a place for making love by turns. Even in his parents' house, where he continued to live, he installed a big double bed in the French taste. While his mother was working at the market and his father, already a pensioner, was at the hippodrome or the cafe, he would receive there the elegant and besotted girls of his retinue. But he wasn't a real skirt-chaser; paradoxically, making love served only to demonstrate the futility of everything.

I had, unfortunately, the highest admiration for him. His impeccable Burberry coats and white shoes, his nihilistic optimism were for me a great model of how to live. And he was fond of me too. In the summer he'd take me to the swimming pools, carrying me on his bike or in a car. Once at the pool, he was soon lost among the bronzed beauties awaiting him. With the aid of one of these girls, he once tossed me into the air and the water, shouting amid his laughter: "You must learn to swim in life, as well!" That day I did learn to swim and was very grateful to him. Then came the incident that made me hate him, and that began the just (or perhaps random) vendetta of fate itself against him.

At that time my mother used to prepare *sciolet* every Friday. That was the best day of the week for me. There was just one little task to be performed, in order to earn such a good dish. On the way back from school, my brothers and I took turns to fetch the saucepan from the communal oven. The distance was only a mile, at most. One Friday it was my turn to carry out this duty, which was a bit of a sweat, but pleasurable at the end of it all. Twenty minutes after the end of lessons, I was already on my way back home. I was crossing Matyas Square when I became aware that a boy of about my own age had begun following me, under the gaze of the Gypsies who were taking the early afternoon air on the benches. At first, he kept well behind me, then gradually began to dog my heels. Not being able to do anything else, I quickened my pace. He did the same. Then, in the middle of the square, he suddenly bounded ahead of me and blocked my way. "What've you got in that pan?" he demanded, with a confident smile. "*Sciolet* ," I replied. "Ah, then you're a filthy Jew," he said calmly. Then he punched the pan so hard that it flew out of my hand. The lid fell off and rolled away, while the *sciolet* poured onto the ground.

I remember that the noise of its falling seemed to announce the end of the world; I stood there petrified and the boy began to laugh in a confused, dull-witted fashion. Strangely enough, my first thought was not for the insult received; that seemed to me pretty anachronistic, in those unlucky post-war years, knowing what sort of end the Nazis had come to. I felt more contempt for it than rage or indignation. But I thought of Mother, of the *sciolet,* of my brothers who this Friday would be deprived of it, and of myself, who hadn't been able to defend such a precious treasure. I picked up the empty saucepan and began to run home, bellowing and weeping under the indifferent eyes of the old Gypsies.

It seemed to me such a long way to the corner of Teleky Square, suffocating as I was with sobs and tears. Suddenly a terrific roar penetrated my ears, almost knocking me senseless. With an acrobatic swerve, Tibor Schreiber drew in to the curb on the saddle of his gleaming BMW. "What have they done to you, my boy?" he cried, pulling off his goggles. I told him what had happened. Tibor grew very serious. "Show me the boy, take me to him straight away!" he ordered, hauling me like a sack onto the fuel tank of his bike. In a flash we were hurtling towards Matyas Square.

The boy was still there, at the corner, as if waiting for us. He was a handsome blond lad, with fine and decisive-looking features. "That's him," I cried to Tibor Schreiber, getting down from the bike. My saviour, still sitting in the saddle, said to me quite solemnly, "Hit him! Go and hit him now!" The boy was leaning against the wall, awaiting his destiny quite calmly, not showing either arrogance or confidence, almost resigned. Or perhaps awaiting my revenge in order to hate me the more. But I wanted to be loved, even by my most pitiless enemy. I hesitated, and Tibor's voice rang out still more imperiously,

97

"These are the criminals who wiped us out. Just remember that!" The more I felt the gravity of the wrong I'd suffered, the more it seemed to me unjust to profit from the reassuring presence of a grown-up as a witness to my revenge. I didn't move. The timid, almost loving eyes of the boy, or so they seemed to me, gazed at me while he swung about against the wall, still pockmarked by the bullets of the war. For the third time, Tibor exhorted me: "If you don't revenge yourself now, one day he might kill you. Get on with it!"

"No," I thought, "I won't wrong a boy who is guilty but now defenceless; perhaps repentant, and in the final reckoning, innocent."

Suddenly I felt myself seized by the shoulders. Tibor Schreiber, jumping down from the saddle, pulled me towards him and began raining slaps and punches on my face with all his might. Through my flowing tears and blood, I saw the furious face of Tibor, the friendly and timid eyes of the boy, the Gypsy women with their big bouncing breasts who ran up curiously. "Try to become a man!" shouted Tibor, starting his BMW and speeding off. I lay bleeding on the ground, until my mother came to fetch me: "My love, my dearest boy, come home. I will make it better," she whispered. I felt my condemnation, and the Cain-like hatred that swelled up within me against that accursed just man who had dared to punish me. I called on God to send him all the misfortunes in this world, and He heard my prayers, leaving me more confused and dismayed than ever.

A few months later there was a big political upheaval in Hungary, recently liberated from the Nazis and now run by

98

a coalition government drawn from various parties. Unexpectedly, one of these parties seized the reins of power, and the new regime also introduced new concepts concerning property, rights and duties, even life itself, in short. Tibor Schreiber seemed at first put out, then alarmed and finally quite determined not to accept these changes, which contrasted so completely with his ideas about human society, born from the humiliating and often terrible experiences of his youth. For him, any form of human solidarity was a lie against which one was bound to rebel. Once again, he chose the opposite sex as the means of his rebellion. Right in these very months, he became officially engaged to a lovely girl from Popular Theatre Street, a tall brunette with big blue eyes who had one fundamental defect, apart from certain aspects of her character: she was a *goyte*, daughter of a porter, a class noted in the Eighth District for their anti-Semitism and for a record as informers against the Jews. Tibor's mother wept bitterly over this engagement.

"To be killed is one thing," she said; "one dies and there's an end. But to destroy with one's own hands all hope for the future, bringing up *goyim* children, that's folly!" I remember the interminable discussions within my numerous family around this by no means new argument, which were such as to draw forth every time a serious religious and philosophical dispute, often culminating in shouts and vows never to set foot again in the house of this or that relation. Tibor, whilst being a good enough Jew so far as his feelings were concerned, certainly didn't observe the laws and precepts of the Talmud; hence, without asking himself too many questions, he declined to break off the engagement. The girl's name was Eve, almost as if to symbolize the risks Tibor was running.

One day I heard from my father that our distant relative had been arrested and sent to a concentration camp as a "class enemy", as they then styled certain elements thought to be dangerous to our new society. Tibor Schreiber, to tell the truth, took no interest in politics; still less would he have risked his own freedom, already bewept through long years of his youth, for the sake of an ideal. He was a practical man; he had simply tried to flee to another country, different from what Hungary then was. I only learned what had really happened after many months of silence on my parents' part. Tibor had bribed the captain of a Hungarian cargo boat which shuttled between Budapest and Vienna, so that he and his fiancée could come aboard and be hidden in the hold, between the grain and the other cargo. Believing himself followed, he had entrusted to Eve all the money and gold objects, apparently of great value, which were intended to secure their future exile. But Eve too had made her own choice: instead of keeping the appointment, she sent the secret police to seize Tibor and kept all his riches for herself. Two months later, she was already married to a *goy* doctor.

For more than a year, nothing more was heard of Tibor Schreiber. His mother, my Aunt Lilli, a woman who had completed barely two years of school but was very sharp and intelligent, put all her acquaintance in motion to obtain even the vaguest, the most discouraging information. But they could get for her no more than a mere assurance that her son was still alive.

I won't say that my ill-will made me delight in the news

100

that filtered in, but neither did it cause me any apprehension for Tibor's fate. "He brought it on himself," I thought, and in my heart, even though not strictly educated in religious observance, I explained all the precepts by this one alone: "He wanted to take a *schikse,* when all the pretty Jewish girls would have given their souls to marry him." On the other hand, in the name of principles which I knew only by hearing them repeated, I condemned Tibor as a parasitic "class enemy". If he didn't believe in anything, I, as often happens, used political faith and ideals simply as instruments to protect my incapacity in life, hoping to prolong that very incapacity, and life itself, indefinitely.

The day came that should have brought my vendetta to a head. Aunt Lilli, after tireless insistence and miles of walking between the offices and houses of officials, after making secret payments for all the time they had lost, managed at last to learn the name of the place where her son was held and get a permit to visit him. For this formidable train journey I was chosen as her companion, perhaps because of my undeserved reputation as a bright, intelligent boy. Tibor's father was seriously ill at the time and none of the adult males in the family dared risk approaching these terrible internment camps. We left at dawn from the South Station and, after passing the whole morning and afternoon in the train, arrived at a village whose name has completely vanished from my memory. I remember the boundary fence, the faces of the three young Gypsies in military uniform who acted as guards, and the severe cleanliness of a room floored with wooden planks. After a while, Aunt Lilli was called by name and taken off

101

towards some other buildings. That day I didn't manage to see the hated figure of Tibor and my joy evaporated. But I was partly compensated by Aunt Lilli's account to the family when we got back. Her son was working in a sawmill. He had lost two teeth from a blow received in punishment for some irreverent comment on the authorities. As he sat down, he had whispered to his mother, "If I ever get out of here, I'll stick a knife in the heart of that *schikse* bitch!"

The day of Tibor Schreiber's liberation came. While everyone else dreaded some fresh wicked act of his, I was already savouring the bloody scene, the uproar, the flight through the Eighth District, the arrival of the police, the arrest and conclusive punishment of my mortal enemy. But Tibor returned to us as a mild, resigned man, truly "re-educated" by four years of forced labour. When he saw me for the first time, he took me on his knees and said to me in a deep, gentle voice, "For you life will be better, my boy. You aren't a *meschügge* like me." This act of benevolent reassurance struck me as disgusting. I wouldn't even take the trouble to ask him why he hadn't "stuck a knife in the heart of that bitch." I closed within myself an image of him as a poor wretch, unworthy even of hatred.

But within a few months the thorn I had thought expelled from my flesh forever began to prick me again, more sorely than before. At the Jewish festivals, now celebrated with less joy and fervour than in the old days, Tibor again turned up with the most beautiful girls on his arm, no longer those in the first flush of youth, but always young and fresh. He put on the sharpest clothes and those "tube" trousers which were stamped as the emblem of

Western bourgeois dress. What's more, Tibor had again found a way of making money and giving full vent to his Don Juan temperament. This time, his mother stuck close to him and, what with preaching and subtle impositions, made sure that Tibor didn't again risk literally losing his teeth at the hands of some *goyte* wench. Such was the energy of this indomitable man that he soon made enough money to frequent the Budapest nightclubs two or three times a week, always in the company of the smartest and most expensive women.

As for his official occupation he was, I think, an electrician, but once his working hours were over he went off with a friend to sell materials. They would pretend to be tourists from Czechoslovakia or Poland, even imitating the accents. Bearing in mind how tightly our borders were closed, and the relatively advanced textile industries of those countries so close to our own, these materials were considered precious. Whilst Tibor had formerly palmed off Czech or Polish stuff as Irish, he now sold cloth made in Hungary itself as being from those countries. This ingenious and basically innocuous trickery, playing upon the foolish desire for distinction, brought him piles of money. Not being able to use it to buy cars, lorries or motorbikes, Tibor employed it exclusively to obtain the best girls in the whole city, provided, however, that they were exclusively Jewish. In those days he had chosen me, for some reason, as his confidant. He told me about all his latest conquests and gave me advice for the future, when I too should begin to take an interest in girls. One day Tibor told me all about how he had won the loveliest dancer in a Budapest nightclub, a certain Jutka. His description was

103

more or less like this: "She has a body that looks like marble, two tits more beautiful than those of the best statue in the world, and eyes as green as two emeralds. I've never seen such a piece of arse. I stuck close to her for two months, then I realized what a pile of money I needed to get her. I promised to maintain her for life if she'd just come to bed with me once. *Sag schon,* how things can turn out later, no?" The girl kept an appointment in a hotel on the Mount of Liberty, but she insisted that Tibor cover his face with a cushion while they copulated; she wanted neither to see his face nor hear his breathing.

Destiny absolved Tibor from lifelong payment for that one, miserable, sickening embrace. There came weeks of disorder, the borders were almost unguarded, and Tibor fled from the Eighth District and from Hungary, along with a fiery little Jewess, the daughter of a former shoemaker, who had been working as a tavern waitress.

I also went away. I met this despised man one December morning in Vienna, on the Kärtnerstrasse. He was much thinner and his eyes, once so gay, now looked burnt-out. Life had fled from his glance, which I remembered as fiery with rage and indignation, reddened with the reflection of my blood. "Life is a disgrace, my son," he said, "my last cunt came here with me and then went off to Argentina, to her uncle. She left me here alone." He made me sad, with his thirty-seven years, passed between prisons and beds all more or less sweaty, with his eternal arid air of non-existent paternity. But above all I wanted to be loved, even by this my mortal enemy! I agreed to help him as an interpreter and accompany him to various offices concerned with

104

immigration and assistance. "Thank you, my boy, you're a good young Jew. Now, do you know what we'll do? We'll go and eat something. *Sag schon,* I shit on this world, it's going to the dogs. I know a place where they make an excellent *sciolet,*" I nearly fainted at the sound of that word. I turned on my heel and left him there in the snow, with his nihilism, his "cunts" and his accursed destiny, thinking that God would soon give him the *coup de grace* and cancel him finally from the face of the earth.

During the following years, in letters from my parents, I sometimes read news of the hated person of Tibor Schreiber. I knew, for example, that he had ended up in Canada, and that in such a neat, well-organized country he hadn't found any occupation adapted to his conception of life. Much more complicated mechanisms than those he was accustomed to operated there, before one could hope to make a profit. One needed a far-sighted mind and the ability to penetrate the most secret habits of possible purchasers. To influence these in the mass required extensive financial means, right from the start. In a letter of my father's written some twenty years ago, it seemed to me that, reading between the lines, Tibor Schreiber had abandoned a series of humiliating jobs in order to take up games of chance and devote himself to the art of card-sharping. "Good enough!" I thought, "that way he's sure to end his days in prison." I was confident that even the women would no longer look him in the face. I forgot him and went my own way, battling painfully against the world and against myself, with the thorn of my own weakness planted in my heart by that swindler of the last order who was Tibor Schreiber, one of the most despicable sons of the Eighth District.

And now comes the epilogue of this disheartening tale. Some fifteen years ago I happened to make a journey to France; I had been invited by an old friend and schoolmate who was working for one of the big Paris publishers. Walking with him one September afternoon in the avenue Kléber with the intention of visiting Proust's house in the nearby rue Hamlin, my attention was attracted by some loud shouts and imprecations. In front of a hotel, The Three Stars, I think, a taxi driver was arguing with a foreigner who was disputing the charge for the trip. This elegant gentleman, so avaricious as to argue about half-a-franc, was Tibor Schreiber, and with him I saw to my astonishment Eve, the beautiful porter's daughter from Popular Theatre Street; the very person who had done him the most frightful injury. I understood in an instant part of what had occurred; the rest I learned from one of my father's letters. Needless to add that, as soon as I saw Tibor, I took to my heels in order to avoid meeting him.

Tibor, then, had risen from the dust by the will of the Almighty. By a stroke of fortune, he had become a partner in a small industry in Ottawa, and in the course of five years, working day and night, had become a substantial citizen, free of all financial worries. Then he had returned to his sometime fiancée Eve, whom he had evidently forgiven, seeing that in him the sentiment of love was always stronger than the desire for justice or revenge. After her divorce and conversion to Judaism, Tibor had married her and put aside for ever all thought of any other "cunts". So, it was all deception; my sufferings had been mere delusions, useless distractions. The Almighty had rewarded

106

all the contradictions of this man, all his tricks, his scepticism and guilty piety; exactly as He had condemned me as an unjust man. When I learned all this of Tibor, I felt within me a desperation impossible to master, an infinite bitterness.

That day, the two tourists who offered me, almost as alms, a spoonful of their *sciolet*, saw me burst into tears at the roadside. I swallowed that food with the same feelings as someone who stretches out his neck for the blow of the axe.

THE CHRISTIANS

Goy: this word was always pronounced among the Jews of the Eighth District with a mixture of indifference and suspicion. To say that someone was a *goy* was like admitting the possibility that he was capable of doing something that a Jew had never done - in a negative sense, naturally. However calmly the word was pronounced, the voice always concealed a certain secular diffidence, a scarcely concealed hostility, repaid in full measure, as far as I remember, by the Christians themselves.

At the market, whenever a quarrel grew up between one of them and a trader, a reference to "stinking Jews" was obligatory. The advanced Christians, as soon as discussion turned to Jewish beliefs, would ask, "But why do you believe in the Messiah?"

And yet even among the Jewish families of the Eighth District there were some Christians, wedged in among their relatives, and still more within domestic life, like extraneous bodies in a living organism. In richer communities perhaps they wouldn't have aroused so much amazement. The big Jewish traders all over the world are accustomed to having Christian servants. It's a shrewd device which permits the overcoming of certain religious prohibitions. On Saturdays, for example, a Jew is not permitted to do any type of work, not even to push the button of an elevator, while a Christian housemaid can perform any necessary task. For those who don't belong to the Chosen People, the observance or flouting of these commandments brings neither help nor harm.

But this was not the reason for the presence of certain Christians in the Eighth District; for in the observance of religious rules there, any strictness had been abandoned for over a generation. Along with the religion were interwoven certain little compromises, affections, conveniences and business practices.

Otto Jakabffy, the decayed nobleman from Transylvania, contracted to marry Selma Grün after the great slump. He was a peaceable man of pleasant aspect, rather quiet; quite the opposite of the image of a nobleman in the eyes of the Hungarian Jews; for the nobility, the cream of the nation, couldn't be expected to live in harmony with the dregs of the country, the pariahs consisting, not of rich bankers, but of petty artisans and traders. Nobility and anti-semitism became synonymous in the Eighth District when the repression of the hundred-day Communist Republic was celebrated by a series of ferocious pogroms. That time - in 1920 - no injuries were done to the Jews of the big market. But frightening news leaked in from the countryside, of whole communities beaten up, synagogues sacked and young Jewish girls raped. The nobles were the masters in the countryside, the black angels of the pogroms. And then, the man in power was Count Admiral Nicholas Horthy, with his white charger; a noble among nobles. Only in 1944 would the Jews have preferred that Horthy remain at the head of the country. When the Admiral declared a separate peace, people danced and wept for joy in the courtyards of the Jewish houses. Five hours later, the head of the local Nazis, Szallasy, who took power with the aid of the German army, annulled every liberal measure. Next day began the Calvary of half a million Jews. They were easily identified; a long-enacted law already required them to wear a yellow Star of David, sewn onto their jackets. Now the roving bands of Nazis ("snotty brats" the Jewish women called them) could easily pick them out and do with them as they wished.

Mr Otto was neither with Horthy nor with Szallasy. For a long time he had renounced demanding anything more than his daily bread. He paid for everything with a slow growth in his intestines. They had to remove one of his kidneys, soon after the war. And a few years later the other kidney also got infected. Then the baronet decided to make an end of it. He threw himself from the hospital window and was dashed to pieces in the garden.

His place was taken by Manci the Gypsy girl, who became an orphan at that very time. Manci and her father lived in the same block as Selma. When she heard that her father had collapsed in a pool of blood in the midst of the tavern where he played the violin every evening, Manci burst into a long fit of crying. Turning her eyes up as if possessed, she groaned, shouted and cursed for an entire day. "That's how it'll be with me," she yelled, tossing about on the chair where the neighbours were tending her. She calmed down when she heard that she would be able to stay in Selma Grün's house. She needed just this type of servant, someone desolate and ready to do anything. Manci put up with the most violent insults and the most

111

degrading instructions. She smothered her rage by murmuring curses in the Romany tongue. And if somebody asked her what the words meant, she would reply, "Nothing, just that I'm dying." Later on, Manci also picked up a bit of Yiddish, and her curses became a mixture of Slav, Hungarian, Romany and Hebrew. She also learned to swear as the Jews do among themselves: "Let me die, then! Let God punish me!"

The Gypsy girl, grown fat on a diet which was after all more abundant than she'd ever had in her life, put up with every type of exertion. The biggest was that of looking after her mistress's body, washing her overflowing, flaccid flesh inch by inch, with towels soaked in a bowl of water; then sprinkling with talcum her ever-sweating skin; treating the varicose veins in her massive legs; combing her hair and training it behind the neck in the antique style; putting on her dark clothes, threadbare with long use, and putting a shawl around her shoulders. Arranged in an armchair, Selma would then be ready to receive the homage of her family every Sunday.

And little by little there grew up between the two women a strange intercourse, which only the intimacy of flesh and spirit could explain. The mistress absorbed from the Gypsy the superstitions and emphatic gestures of the nomads. Manci developed a heavy body, though less so than her mistress, and began to take an interest in petty business. When Selma fell ill, the Gypsy nursed her night and day, without ever uttering a word of consolation, but without leaving her for even an hour. And when she died, Manci seemed like her reincarnation. During the funeral it even seemed to me that Selma was accompanying her own coffin, so much did Manci resemble her - the same wrinkles of rage, the hard look, the same severe hairstyle and deportment.

The Gypsy set up house in the apartment left vacant by the dead woman, even taking over her clothes and entering into the traffic which her mistress had established with the countryside. She received butter, meat and eggs in exchange for cloth, buttons and articles of common use. Later she enlarged her trade to take in the Poles and Czechs who visited the city. She would even have liked to assume Selma's former authority over the Gypsies, but they just laughed in her face. It was a row with a neighbour, a double-bass player, which settled everything. Manci yelled exactly as her mistress had done so many times. In vain. The Gypsies of the block, even if a bit alarmed, smothered her with insults. After that, she no longer spoke to people of her race, upon whom her prodigious metamorphosis had no effect.

Juliet, the wetnurse of Erdeli Street, was even more unfortunate than Manci. She had been a servant all her life and knew no other role. Her consolation was her faith. She went to Mass every morning. An hour later, when Rachel's children woke up, she was ready with the coffee and milk. Even in the days when no one would have advised frequenting the church, she remained devoted to Saint Rita, whose chapel was close by. She had no religious problem so far as the Jews were concerned; she called down the blessing of the saints on them too. She was certain that the good Lord heard their prayers also. In the evening she retired to the basement of the block. There she prayed before a sacred image which never lacked the glory

of a lighted candle. She never spoke of her past. With the
children and the world in general she was always patient,
and, unlike Manci, quite free of any ambition. Her long
years gradually melted away without leaving a trace. Just
as if she had never lived. The wheels of a tram tore her
body apart one evening when she was wandering
distractedly in the road.

But no one was more unlucky than Louis, the porter in
the main market. Dressed in rags, with drooping
moustache and eyes always bright from drinking, Louis
couldn't even talk. He could only indicate approval or
disapproval with raucous, inarticulate gutteral sounds. For
a few coins, he would carry away the remains of the
poultry and vegetables brought into the city by the
peasants. Once his work was over, he went to the tavern.

The Jews have a strong dislike for the vice of
drunkenness. And this was the trait that distinguished the
rejected sons of David from those of the Christians.
Workers, porters, prostitutes, the unemployed, would hang
about every afternoon in the Eighth District taverns; dirty,
smoky places, where sadness, oaths and brawls were the
order of the day. Unwashed curtains on the windows hid
from the passersby those who drank there. Daily fights on
the pavement resolved with blows and bloodshed the
quarrels born at the counter. One tavern had been made in
the depths of a cellar. Despite ten steep steps, difficult to
climb with a spinning head, this place was popular with
the boozers. They felt they were in the belly of the earth,
imagining themselves already damned and in hell. Little did
it matter if they broke their noses when coming up again.
Neither did they recognize that the ominous darkness of

the place, the porcelain tiles like those of a toilet, matched the hard, invincible desperation that held them there.

Louis had left even despair behind him. Nothing in life counted for him any more; he was, like a saint, the least of the human beings in the Eighth District. For him there was no hell, no heaven, no beyond, no home, no relations, no faith, no promises. There was only his grievous body wounded with privations; his big, blackened hands; his bright, clouded eyes; and the passing days killed with alcohol. Nothing more.

The Jews had miraculously comprehended his sanctity, coarse and wretched traders as they were. Louis was the only Christian permitted to enter their temple for the most solemn ceremonies and the *bar-mizvà* of some of the local teenagers. He stopped at the last bench and gazed smilingly at the pulpit, where the Torah was being read. He seemed to understand words pronounced in Hebrew, perhaps exactly because they must have been quite incomprehensible to him. They found him dead one winter morning, in a corner of the market, covered with an old overcoat full of holes; a mouldy, patched bearskin hat on his head.

His funeral was the most splendid in the District. Behind the hearse, drawn by four black horses, came a Gypsy orchestra, all paid for by Selma Grün, playing both solemn and jolly music. And behind the Gypsies walked the market Jews, the women muffled up in shapeless topcoats, the men with caps pulled down to the tops of their long noses. That was how the porter Louis went to his long home; an unnamed tomb in the remotest corner of the cemetery in Kerepes Road. The Jews of the quarter had thought of ordering an impressive burial service; but, of obtaining a cross to place above the tomb, no, certainly not.

NATHAN

Nathan's journey began and ended - if such things have beginnings and endings - one summer evening, when the stars were piercing the soul with fear. It was performed without a passport or any other preparations; without either hopes or intentions. Not even he, Nathan, had expected to arrive so far away and with such amazing facility. He was the rebel, and the opponent of this poor pale Jew of the Eighth District was the Almighty Himself, may His Name be Blessed, in all His splendour and all His inscrutability.

"No preparations," I said. Nathan had certainly done nothing consciously to become the protagonist of this adventure. However, looked at more closely, his whole life had been a preparation for nothing else.

I remember him as a boy. He used to walk pallidly through the streets still marked by the cruelty of war. He had heard the last bombardments when delirious with fever and tortured by lung disease. His skinny body was draped with a heavy overcoat, inherited from an elder brother, while a huge scarf, wrapped around his neck by an apprehensive mother, hid his face from the eyes of the curious. He was the sickliest child in the quarter and in his soul, right from his infancy, moments of extreme

117

discouragement or tormented gloom would abruptly change to those of unrestrained joy and vitality. More than once I have found him slumped on a school bench, fallen in upon himself, as if the very structure of his bones and vital forces had collapsed. He would gaze sullenly into space, indifferent to everything around him. In his third year of elementary school - he was not more than ten years old - his brow was already scored with three horizontal lines, deep and conspicuous, which looked strange upon that smooth, boyish face. "Don't wrinkle your forehead when you talk, you'll grow old before your time," our schoolmistress Margaret would tell him, for she attributed these creases simply to a bad habit. How could the teacher imagine what they really hid? As a matter of fact, Nathan didn't screw up his brow without reason; he found talking an extreme exertion, and the phrases he uttered were doubtful and brief.

He was the child of petty traders, the Slovak innkeeper Ionter and his wife Deborah, and hadn't received a good education. Sometimes his father would bring home an old book. He was especially fond of novels, and used to offer these as reading to his son. "Have to get yourself a bit of culture," he would say to Nathan. The characters of these novels, which included the masterpieces of literature from Tolstoy to Flaubert, paraded before Nathan's memory as if in flesh and blood, becoming part of his daily life: insignificant, incomprehensible and absurd. Page after page was shed into his memory, and volumes piled on volumes. But the book of life remained closed to him.

Nathan refused to think. He was alarmed by the abyss of thought. When he found himself on the precipice of an intuition, he would quickly move backward, as if to say: "Why should this mystery be revealed to me? Who am I?" He was afraid of glimpsing terrible truths or forbidden visions, of drawing upon himself severe punishments or even eternal damnation. Or was it simply a mixture of his own laziness and cowardice? I can't say.

The pale boy became, then, a diligent book-keeper. But no more than that. Just as a job, one might say. If there was one mystery that aroused less fear in him than others, it was the reading of the laws of numbers. Nathan applied that knowledge with skill and ease, devising ingenious demonstrations in trigonometry and algebra while he was still at school. Even there, he refrained from exploring fields still unknown to him, but no one could equal him in performing calculations. When he was presented with a problem, he would prove and reprove his answer until he arrived, perhaps more by chance than intuition, at the correct solution. He would fill page after page, sitting up late into the night, and only after many days of fruitless effort would he leave off the task, attracted by some new calculation, some new problem to work on.

When he finished his schooling, he broke off with the family also. He went to live in a distant quarter, near the edge of the city. A room and a kitchen in the hive of a new estate offered him shelter, and a job in a big food-producing firm occupied his days. His mother hadn't wanted to let him go, perhaps because she feared losing control over him. But Nathan insisted that now he was grown up he needed to make his own life, and that the job required him to move anyway; otherwise he'd have to spend three hours a day in the tram, between his parents' house and the office.

To move house he needed only a suitcase full of clothes and linen. The bed, wardrobe, table and chairs were quite cheaply bought. Nathan added a second-hand divan and a bookcase for the few books he possessed. All this happened soon after 1956, the year in which Nathan lost many of his friends, some of whom went to America, some to Germany and some to Israel. As for his contacts with the Jewish community, these had almost entirely ceased. The great turmoil of that year left no other trace on his soul than a still greater solitude, the thinning-out of friendly faces around him, the obligation to form new habits. Looking after the apartment engaged him only once a week, for a few hours. He took his washing to one of the laundries which abounded in that quarter, remade his bed on Sundays and barely rinsed his coffee cup every morning. He lunched in small restaurants with his meal tickets and contented himself with a cold supper at night.

So his years passed. Of his former love for mathematics, he was left with only a sterile aspiration. For that, Nathan substituted an interest in music. He took up the guitar and read some books on harmony and composition. He spent hours plucking at the strings; he also tried playing the flute, and sometimes the piano. He had bought an old one from a family left without children. His fingers were timid, like his thoughts, and inexpert, yet they could dream of blazing chords, rapid cascades of notes, clusters of shifting assonances. But still Nathan did not become a musician.

He was always short of time for everything, never finding the right way to realize his aspirations. He put off the commitments proposed by his own fantasy, for a month, a year, or until conditions were more favourable. And all the time, in the office, he counted and measured, corrected columns of figures, won little promotions and small rewards. He maintained only sporadic contacts with his family, while love brushed against him only in silent encounters which gave little pleasure to the woman. His appearance, even as an adult, remained what it had always been; clothes always too dark and too large for him; his body almost hidden beneath them. Beyond this, Nathan hid himself as far as he could; he spoke in a tiny voice, almost a whisper; and his expression always wore a veil of fixity, betraying neither interest nor emotion. All this gave an impression of profound, impenetrable melancholy; the kind of melancholy which, if it remains passive, condemns one to a monotonous and anguished existence; but if it takes on the fire of ecstasy, exalts the heart and fills the head with prophecies and marvellous visions, such as to bring new light to mankind. When the flute, the guitar and the piano of Nathan fell silent, his soul turned towards an interest in the philosophy of ancient peoples. During long evenings at the Szecheny Library, he leafed through scholarly editions of Epicurus, Plato and Aristotle, while the afternoon sun paled outside, or it rained, or snowed, or the sun came out again, all depending upon the cycle of the seasons.

Sometimes Nathan travelled abroad. He visited Prague and Venice, along with millions of other people. He lost himself among the monuments and the throng. These cities stimulated his nostalgia and imagination. He dreamed of living there, and tried to conjure up a life for himself among the lagoons, among these swarming and rowdy people, among these Italians who had none of the acid hostility shown by certain Hungarians towards the whole world, nor the Jews' crazy fear of God, of fate and of time. Then he went back to the Szecheny Library, to his untidy flat, to the penetrating odour of dust and mould.

Around him he saw people who planned their Sundays and their travels, built themselves houses beside lakes or rivers, bought cars or tape recorders, dreaming of a terrestrial paradise in which it was enough just to want something. "Like everywhere else," I told him, during one of our encounters, "and anyway, why shouldn't it be so? To have or to be are ridiculous alternatives." It was during his visit to Venice that Nathan accomplished his final metamorphosis. In the synagogues, in the alleys of the former ghetto, in the old library there, among those venerable volumes, he recognized himself as the son of an ancient people. "What have I done up to now?" he asked himself, more in astonishment than in fear. He had thrown away his own self, renouncing and then seeking himself again where he could not be found. He spoke with an old rabbi in his mangled German. He was asked how it was that he didn't know a word of Hebrew or Yiddish, how he had failed to study the Scriptures and had let himself grow up like a wild thistle, bent here and there by the wind. I saw he had been shaken after this encounter. He had taken from the rabbi the address of a scholarly Jew in Budapest; he bought himself dictionaries and books in order to learn the tongue of his fathers. "I want to speak it," he said, "only when I've become fluent for ever in the language." The rabbi was one of the few Italian scholars who were familiar in our time with the *Zohar*, the Book of Splendours, which contains the finest flower of the cabbala; the "tradition" in more immediate terms; the most profound meditations upon God, the universe, the role of man in the world, and his ability to influence it for good or ill. "It's perilous for anyone to encounter the *Zohar* before passing the middle of his life," said the old doctor, "he could go mad and lose himself forever in its depths." And then he turned to Nathan: "But you are already well past the middle of your life. If you want to learn something of the Eternal Mysteries, may they be blessed, it is time for you to open your eyes and your mind."

We went to Mantua together, to consult in the library there the first printed edition of the Book of Splendours. The big folio emanated a terrible fascination. Between the lines set with such love by the Jewish printer of the sixteenth century were various annotations, additions and glosses written in the margins by unknown commentators. A whole rabbinical school, composed of many generations of scholars, must have watched over these volumes.

Nathan burnt his wings, like a moth in the heat of a lamp, in the blaze of the mysteries partially revealed to him by the Venetian rabbi. He made me promise to send or bring personally to Budapest the six volumes of the *Zohar* in French translation; the only edition in a European language of this most feared of cabbalistic books. "I want to lose myself in those mysteries," he told me. "If I have the strength, I'll dedicate the rest of my life to that." I saw in his eyes the flame of a fever so intense that I didn't dare contradict him. I bought the books for him with the greatest care; six black volumes printed in a limited edition, costly and austere. Before consigning them to their owner, during my brief stay in Budapest, I leafed through them, without understanding much of the French text. I glimpsed through the words a distant, astral world, but nothing more. My imagination lay cold, like a stopped engine. I was little impressed, or so it seemed to me at the time, by the almost prophetic analysis of the absolute, the creation, and divinity itself. These are not matters upon which man can argue, I thought. But it was just then that Nathan's journey began.

Nathan took the volumes of the *Zohar* in his hands and began to read them with a terrible avidity. He spent thirty days and thirty nights with them, without rest or sleep. He scribbled his own annotations incessantly upon the pages.

Before writing on them, he soaked the pages in water. "It's the only way to be sure they don't burn in the fire of the mysteries," he said. He wrote page after page, all in Hebrew characters, just as he had formerly done with numbers and with notes of music. These were attempts made without ordered preparation, with only a blind persistence. As many stars as there are in the most splendid of summer nights, so many were the possible combinations of the letters Nathan wrote on his pages. As numerous as the years of eternity, as long as the file of souls of those who had lived and died from the moment of creation, so long and so many times would he have to write that number in order to strike the prophetic version.

The whole universe seemed to resist his efforts with horrible tenacity. Sleep paralysed Nathan's mind and hands, just to prevent his speaking or hearing. He discouraged visits by friends or acquaintances in order to fulfil his task. His eyelids might seal themselves up and his hands fall slack at any moment. Thirty times thirty thoughts were locked as if in a frozen lake: thirty times thirty sweet dreams were replaced by others desperate with the blackest despair. But Nathan didn't give up. He wouldn't give way to sleep, to paralysis, to the flight of his thoughts or the weakness of his body. "Keep on!" a voice cried within him, "Don't tire, don't stop now!" But other voices whispered to him, "Sleep, give it up now, rest." He longed to weep and rid himself of his incubus. But from it there could be no release.

When by chance he saw on his pages the name that unsealed the fifty-first doorway of the heavens, the paper caught fire. Nathan himself felt for a moment as though he had burned his hand, then his arm, then his heart, like one who has been struck by lightning. He remembered that moment with brilliant clarity. Then a soft light wrapped around him, making him forget the weight and resistance of nature. He floated through this light and drank the dew of the heavens. "Tremble, for you are walking towards the radiance of the Lord," said a familiar voice, that of Cantor Stern, who had taught him to read Hebrew, when his mind was judged mature enough. "Tremble, because you are climbing towards the most secret door of the skies, the encounter with the sacred host of angels and great and hallowed rabbis."

Nathan climbed for a long while upon the holy trunk of the sephirotic tree, the tree which bore the whole immense creation, the emanation of the Lord, may His Name be Blessed, and the more he climbed, the more the light became ever purer and softer and imperceptible and more benevolent. His ascent became ever lighter and more buoyant. Until they threw open for him the door of the chamber where the celestial assembly was taking place. An indescribably beautiful and serene music floated forth, a pale echo of which he had heard in the temple, when the little bells tinkled on the vestments of the Torah.

The angels were all ranged before him, and to Nathan it was permitted to drink from the Fount of Eternity.

"Who is this who dares come here while still carrying the impure shade of the living?" bellowed a voice, that of the terrible and sanctified Rabbi Akiba, Luminary of Creation, incomparable jewel in the Chamber of the Lord, may His Name be Blessed. Nathan heard him with deep emotion, yes, but without any fear, since no fear could exist in the chamber of that celestial assembly. Meanwhile the angels began to whisper among themselves and repeat the question of the blessed rabbi, stupefied and amazed at such audacity. And Rabbi Simeon now said: "Who dares to imitate me in my mortal form?" "It is I, Nathan, from the Eighth District of Budapest," the guest promptly replied, in a clear, sharp voice, quite free from any mortal fear.

"Let us see what mystery of the universe and what passage of the Scriptures you have come to expound to our meeting; what verse upon which we have meditated countless times," demanded Rabbi Simeon.

"I have not come here to explain any verses; my mind is not sufficiently gifted with acumen and profundity," replied Nathan without shame.

"So, how do you dare show yourself?" growled Rabbi Akiba again, joined now by Yokai, Eliezer son of Simeon, and Mirquia.

126

"Blessed and hallowed rabbis, I understand your indignation, since you have spent your earthly lives bent over the word of the Scriptures, to penetrate its depths and reveal its true meaning to the world. Nevertheless, the Holy One, may His Name be Blessed, has reserved in His infinite bounty one secret door in His High Palace for someone who is not of the elect and holy, like yourselves, blessed angels and rabbis. That door of the Creation will be opened to whatever being, excepting demons or evil angels, has wished to write the fifty-first name of the Lord. And so access here, by the infinite bounty of the Most High, may His Name be Blessed, is not denied even to a humble, still-living man in his earthly flesh, such as I am, because it is written in that secret order 'whatever being'. Do not marvel then at my presence here in your sacred assembly, and do not ask me for explanations of verses in the Scriptures, which I certainly cannot offer to your High Spirit."

"Why do you come to disturb us?" cried an angel from the ranks.

"The Most High, in His bounty, may His Name be Blessed, has left this possibility even to someone who has not performed works of particular merit, for the splendour of the palace can be known by means of chance messengers, even in the world below, even to one who can never aspire to enter it in his own right. And all this for His Greater Glory and to spur men onward in labour for the accomplishment of the Great Work. But injustice cannot be performed in the presence of the just. He has hidden the key of the door so well, that to the unworthy there remains only one tiny, infinitesimal possibility of

127

finding it. The door could have remained shut until the End of Days, if I had not found the key. And I found it, not by merit, which I do not possess, but in the troubled search for my identity, which the Most High, may His Name be Blessed, had hidden from me all my life. By sheer force of searching I have thus stumbled upon what I had no hope of finding."

A murmur of amazement and admiration went up from the assembly at this explanation of Nathan's. And Rabbi Simeon declared: "But now that you are here, what do you wish to do with your carnal presence? What do you hope to accomplish, which can be fruitfully employed in the world below, during the life that remains to you?"

"Nothing," replied Nathan, "but the occasion offers me the possibility of posing one question."

"What question can you ask, who have allowed the mist of ignorance and iniquity to flourish in your sight, and have not performed one action to dispel it and enlighten your mind, to increase in you the love of the Almighty, may His Name be Blessed, your Lord and Creator?"

So tolled the voice of Rabbi Simeon.

"Oh sacred Rabbi Simeon," exclaimed Nathan, "why didn't you live in my century, so I could have known you before. Why didn't you live in the Eighth District, where moral wretchedness and physical filth vie with each other to hide from us the face of the Lord? Then you could have taught the True Way to those people. And I could have seen how high you would have risen, hidden in that place and in those conditions. Perhaps you think the Exile in Egypt was more bitter and humiliating than our exile in Teleky Square? Are you convinced that the sins of our people were worse than those committed in the times and in the sight of Moses in the desert? The Lord, may His Name be Blessed, flung us into the Eighth District so that our hearts might be tested. Who can resist the power of the Lord? Our eyes were fixed, as long as we could hold them, upon the Sacred Presence. We were mocked and tried, we lost our language, and unhappiness spread amongst us; whilst money and daily living brought worries that sapped our strength. Then the Lord, to punish us, sent the Exterminating Angel over our heads, and our fathers were enslaved worse than in Babylon, and when, worn out, they were of no further use, they were burned in the gas chambers. Oh Rabbi, are you surprised that after this punishment many of us left off for long years our contribution to the Great Work of the Lord, may His Name be Blessed, lying inert and useless like stunned flies? But still some of us, in our small way, strove to reanimate ourselves and take our fate into our own hands. I know that we are in the world to serve the Lord's Work, just as machines were invented by man to serve him. Like machines, we don't know the real purpose, the real end of our existence. What engine can guess why his passenger wants to get off in one place or another? So are we ignorant about the inscrutable intentions of the Lord. And yet we busy ourselves to complete the part of the Work entrusted to us, and whoever loses sight of his own part, whoever fails to recognize the orders given him at birth, will then strive to find them for the rest of his life, until he is struck down by the Angel of Death."

So spoke Nathan to his elevated audience, and then fell silent to listen. The ranks of angels looked with pity upon

129

the plight of the mortal before them, and one of them asked what was the question he wanted to put. Then Nathan said:

"Look down there, upon the Eighth District, at that swarm of wretched beings, blighted with madness and disease, condemned to ignorance and affliction. Look at the fruit brought forth by the Tree of Israel! I want to know the reason for so much pain and so much suffering. I want to know what's the sense of it all, where our road is leading, what fate awaits us poor creatures of the most afflicted district in the world."

A thunderous shout seemed to shatter Nathan's eardrums.

"Don't you know what you're saying? You are calling into question what is written in the Book!"

"Why are only holy rabbis permitted to speak in this assembly, and why must a humble Jew like me be silenced?" replied Nathan.

It was then that a mysterious and fascinating voice, one different from any heard on earth, became audible to Nathan:

"Poor son of the Eighth District! But now that by your efforts the fifty-first door has been opened and a secret has been disclosed, you may reveal other secrets and set yourself before the Great Book, so that you may read it and grasp whatever your miserable mind is capable of grasping."

At this moment such a splendour as no human eye has ever perceived was beheld by Nathan. He saw the rows of all the Eighth District Jews exterminated in the Holocaust, seated side by side in white vestments, those very

130

vestments in which the funeral rites would have robed them if they had not been killed and burned in the extermination camps. Then Nathan saw his own ancestors, men with long beards, and stooping women. They surrounded him and sang songs unknown to him, brushing against his shoulders and his temples. Nathan's knees shook as he greeted them one by one. The faces of the ancestors now enabled him to trace the marvellous transformations worked by nature. He saw distant forefathers of squat stature and swarthy looks. He saw the traits of fathers and mothers merging into those of their children. He saw the faces changing, mingling, modulating to and from a common matrix across the centuries; he saw also their souls and their minds, in shifting forms and structures. For everything is written in the Book, as in the most wonderful projects of engineering; everything is manifest and clear, as if to its Maker, may His Name be Blessed; everything is clear to the very beginning of the ages.

And the pages of the Book turned under Nathan's eyes, with letters and phrases he struggled to understand. The future was revealed to him.

All this was told to me by Nathan himself. With burning eyes, he drew close to my face and whispered: "I can't reveal all the secrets. I can only tell you that towards us the Most High, may His Name be Blessed, is especially good. Our streets and our squares will become a paradise. I see a time when the Jews, descendants of those who were tortured and exterminated, will be fertile once more. The Eighth District, now old and desolate, will be repopulated, flowers will burst forth and minds will be illuminated with wisdom. The Jews of the quarter and their children will live in peace. The children of the street will know the mysteries of the world as well as the most learned rabbis elsewhere; the women will have glances gentler than those of newly suckled lambs; and the stalls of the goose-dealers will become arbours where nectar is poured forth. It will be one great palace, the Eighth District, full of perfumed gardens and many-coloured flowerbeds. All this is as a gift for the times of suffering and humiliation, the long years of darkness and misery that the people of this quarter have endured. For the Lord giveth and the Lord taketh away. Whoever is ignorant shall enjoy wisdom, whoever has been abandoned in sickness or in madness shall become whole, whoever has been tormented by the demons of poverty shall live in plenty."

That's what Nathan told me. And I cannot doubt his words...

About the translator: Gerald Moore read English at Cambridge University and taught for many years in Africa. He was at the School of African and Asian Studies at Sussex University from 1966 to 1977. His books include *The Chosen Tongue* (1969), *Wole Soyinka* (1978) and *Twelve African Writers* (1980). He has published translations of Mongo Beti and Tchicaya U Tam'si. He co-edited *The Penguin Book of Modern African Poetry* (1984). His much acclaimed translation of the Congolese writer Henri Lopes' *The Laughing Cry* was published by Readers International in 1987. He now lives in Italy with his wife and son.